FOREVER
for US

CARRIE ANN
NEW YORK TIMES BESTSELLING AUTHOR
RYAN

FOREVER FOR US

THE WILDER BROTHERS
BOOK EIGHT

CARRIE ANN RYAN

Forever For Us
A Wilder Brother Novel
By: Carrie Ann Ryan
© 2024 Carrie Ann Ryan

Cover Art by Sweet N Spicy Designs

All content warnings are listed on the book page for this book on my website.

PRAISE FOR CARRIE ANN RYAN

"Count on Carrie Ann Ryan for emotional, sexy, character driven stories that capture your heart!" – Carly Phillips, NY Times bestselling author

"Carrie Ann Ryan's romances are my newest addiction! The emotion in her books captures me from the very beginning. The hope and healing hold me close until the end. These love stories will simply sweep you away." ~ NYT Bestselling Author Deveny Perry

"Carrie Ann Ryan writes the perfect balance of sweet and heat ensuring every story feeds the soul." - Audrey Carlan, #1 New York Times Bestselling Author

"Carrie Ann Ryan never fails to draw readers in with passion, raw sensuality, and characters that pop off the page. Any book by Carrie Ann is an absolute treat." – New York Times Bestselling Author J. Kenner

"Carrie Ann Ryan knows how to pull your heart-strings and make your pulse pound! Her wonderful Redwood Pack series will draw you in and keep you reading long into the night. I can't wait to see what comes next with the new generation, the Talons. Keep them coming, Carrie Ann!" –Lara Adrian, New York Times bestselling author of CRAVE THE NIGHT

"With snarky humor, sizzling love scenes, and brilliant, imaginative worldbuilding, The Dante's Circle series reads as if Carrie Ann Ryan peeked at my personal wish list!" – NYT Bestselling Author, Larissa Ione

"Carrie Ann Ryan writes sexy shifters in a world full of passionate happily-ever-afters." – *New York Times* Bestselling Author Vivian Arend

"Carrie Ann's books are sexy with characters you can't help but love from page one. They are heat and heart blended to perfection." *New York Times* Bestselling Author Jayne Rylon

Carrie Ann Ryan's books are wickedly funny and deliciously hot, with plenty of twists to keep you guessing. They'll keep you up all night!" USA Today Bestselling Author Cari Quinn

"Once again, Carrie Ann Ryan knocks the Dante's Circle series out of the park. The queen of hot, sexy, enthralling paranormal romance, Carrie Ann is an author not to miss!" *New York Times* bestselling Author Marie Harte

CHAPTER ONE
WYATT

"Wyatt! Wyatt, wake up, brother. Wake up."

I blinked open my eyes, the world coming into sharp focus for a second before blurring back out. My head ached, my eyes shutting once again.

What the hell happened?

"That was my question to you," Brooks said.

I hadn't realized I spoke aloud until I heard my brother's reply and the worry laced through his tone.

"Yes, you're still speaking aloud. And not slurring, so I guess you don't have a concussion. Or maybe you do, and since I'm not a doctor I should stop trying to diagnose you. Can you open your eyes for me? Come on, come on, I'm going to get someone to call an ambulance."

I shook my head, not wanting to deal with an ambulance, and immediately groaned, clutching my temples. "Okay, note to self, don't shake your head."

Brooks mumbled something under his breath that I couldn't hear over the scrabbling of somebody else entering the bar.

That's right. I was in my bar. The one that I owned with my family. I slowly sat up, my eyes opening again to see my older brother Brooks kneeling in front of me, holding out his hands.

"Okay, take it easy. You want to tell us what happened?"

I winced as I put my hand on my ribs and cursed. "I don't know. Someone came at me from behind. Hit me in the head. But I think I blocked it partially?" I asked, and then looked down at the newly forming bruise on my forearm. "I don't think it's broken, but fuck that's going to hurt if it's already bruising."

"And you touched your ribs too. He got you there?"

"I think a kick?" I asked.

"Are you asking us, or do you know?" my other brother, Ridge, said, as he frowned, phone in hand. "I called 911. They're sending an ambulance and the police, because somebody fucking attacked you. On our property."

I sighed at Ridge's words, but knew he was right. He and Trace were in charge of security on the Wilder property. Our family owned and operated it, but we all took our jobs seriously. Ridge had to protect the entire property, all the guests on the resort, winery, and distillery, and keep us organized.

He was going to blame himself for this, just like I blamed myself. Of course, before I could do that, I had to get my head back to its original size and stop seeing double.

"Whatever happened is not your fault," I offered, and Ridge narrowed his gaze.

"It's cute you think I'm going to let you say something like that. Did they take anything?" Ridge asked, and my eyes widened before I tried to scramble up and look around.

Sharp pains shot through my side and my breath came in pants. "Fuck."

"Don't hurt yourself."

"You say that as if I have a choice," I mumbled, annoyed, then realized what was missing from beside me. "Hell. I think they took the money bag."

"Fuck," Brooks whispered, as he forced me to keep sitting.

"You had the money bag out?" Ridge asked, glaring at me.

I held up one hand, the other still on my ribs. Maybe if I put enough pressure on them, they wouldn't hurt so much. As another sharp pain sliced through me, I realized that wasn't the case. I didn't think anything was broken, because I'd had broken a rib before, and this didn't feel quite as bad. It still hurt like a bitch.

"Most of it is in the safe; I had one out to put in the other safe. I was closing up. The door was locked." I frowned. "At least I think it was locked."

This time Ridge's neck went red in anger. "What the hell, man?"

"Isabelle and Aaron showed up. They needed to talk." I grimaced. "And she wanted to hand over the divorce papers. I'm pretty sure I locked it after they left."

Brooks gave me a look, and I knew we would be talking about the divorce papers later, and Ridge went over to the door.

"I didn't notice when we first came in, because we saw you on the ground when we looked through the window, but it looks like somebody jimmied the door, so it was locked and they got in without breaking the door. That's something we're going to fucking fix later."

Ridge pulled out his phone again and I knew he was calling Trace, or maybe Aurora, his fiancée.

I was tired, achy, and still so damn confused about what happened.

"Did they take anything else?" I asked, pinching the bridge of my nose.

"It looks like they just beat the shit out of you and

took that bag. But we'll do a full review to be sure. Hell, brother, you look like shit."

I squinted up at him. "I really hate you right now."

"You do. But I hear the sirens, so someone will be able to take care of you who's not me. We both know I'm not good at that."

The police and paramedics showed up moments later, and while I didn't need to ride in the back of an ambulance, I did go to a hospital to get checked out.

I was tired, sore, needed three stitches on the back of my head, and got lots and lots of ice.

"No broken ribs, no concussion, you're just going to be sore for a little while," my doctor said.

"Thanks, Doc. Really wasn't how I wanted to spend my evening. I'm sure you didn't want to do this either."

My doctor shrugged and smiled. "This is my job. I don't mind it. I do mind people being hurt, but that's why I'm here. Now, there're a couple cops outside this door who want to talk to you. You up for that?" he asked.

I leaned back against the pillows and sighed.

"Don't really have a choice. But I want to find out who did this. And who robbed my place."

"The things people will do for money."

"If it was somebody who was broke and hurt and needed something? That's one thing. But they didn't need to knock me out to do it, you know?" I said.

"I see a lot of people come in here who need help, and I get that. Let's just hope it's some person who has everything and wants something more, and not someone who truly needs help."

I shook my head, holding back a laugh because everything hurt. "That's one way to think about it."

"I try. You also have a few guys who look just like you out there, want me to send them in?"

"Send as many as the nurses will allow because I know you have limits on these rooms."

The doctor gave me a two-fingered salute as the nurses laughed beside us and soon Ridge and my cousin Eli were in the room with us, followed by two cops.

"Am I going to need a lawyer?" I asked, and one of the cops raised a brow.

"Not unless you have something to hide."

"I can get LJ out here in a minute," Eli said, looking me over. "You look like hell."

"That is a common consensus. Makes me feel all warm and cuddly inside."

"We just want to know what happened so we can get the person that did it. You're not in trouble here," Cop Number Two said, but Cop Number One kept scowling. Did he think I did this to myself? I wasn't going to ask and antagonize him though. I just tried not to look like I was in pain.

I wasn't in much pain right now because of the good drugs I got earlier.

"So, tell us what happened."

"I was closing up shop and I heard someone behind me. I thought I was alone, and had locked the door, and the bat or whatever to the head hurt like hell."

"Got hit with a bat?" Ridge asked.

"I don't know what it was. I don't think it was an actual bat. Something cylindrical, didn't break my arm thankfully. And they didn't seem to use all their strength in the hit, or I might be dead right now."

Eli cursed as I did my best to make light of the situation. Mostly because that had been scary as fuck.

"So, walk me through your night," Cop Two ordered, as Cop One continued to glower.

"We had a good night, made good money, sold a lot of beer and vodka. I was closing up, because I live on property so it just makes sense for me to do so my team can get home at a reasonable hour. I don't know who did it. Maybe it was just somebody who needed the money. I just wish they wouldn't have hurt me in the process."

"So you were alone. No one else came after your last customer? What time was that?"

"My ex-wife Isabelle and Aaron, her fiancé, showed up after the last customer."

Eli gave me a sharp look while Ridge sighed. Great, I was going to have so many amazing conversations later.

"What time was that?"

"About ten minutes after closing? I don't know. I didn't look at the exact time, but it couldn't have been long after because I was still there."

"And what did they have to talk about? Do you talk with your ex-wife often?"

I snorted, but then winced at the fiery pain in my side. "No. Sorry, laughing hurts. I was waiting for her to sign the divorce papers. She was dropping them off." I frowned. "They should still be somewhere in the bar. She said she forwarded it to the lawyers, and I don't really want to go through that again."

"We'll handle it," Ridge said, and I had a feeling he was going to handle it thoroughly.

"And what time did they leave?"

"About ten minutes after that. And I did lock the door behind them. I'm not imagining that."

"It looked like the lock was jimmied. So, you're saying that your ex-wife and her current fiancé stopped over out of the blue. Does that happen often?" Cop One asked.

"No. I just said it didn't. That's the first time they'd been into my bar, and I don't plan on ever seeing them again. It's over."

"So you guys didn't divorce amicably?"

I laughed then, letting the pain blaze through me. "No, we didn't. But neither of them were ever violent. I caught them cheating, and I broke it off. Now we're finally divorced, and I don't have that weighing over me. They didn't do this."

"We're going to want their information."

That was going to be annoying as hell, but I pulled out my phone.

"This is what I have. I don't know whose house they're living at." Wasn't that just a kick in the balls. But I wasn't hurting from the divorce or even the cheating as much as I probably should have been.

"I don't think it was them. Maybe it was someone who just needed a hand up."

"Are you aware that there've been a few other break-ins in the vicinity?"

I blinked as Eli stood at attention.

"No, that would've been nice to know due to our properties being connected," my cousin said.

He was the CEO of the Wilder Retreat and Winery. We were a huge company, with a spa, two restaurants, a full winery, an inn, and a wedding venue. Between my six cousins and two of my three brothers, we ran the place like a well-oiled machine. And we were known in the community. It was odd that Eli hadn't known about the other break-ins.

"We were going to call your head of security, Trace Pritchett?"

"I'm Ridge Wilder, I'm co-head of security now. So we can talk about it."

"We can do that. Have you seen a Mr. Zach Green recently?" Cop One asked, his voice gravelly.

I frowned and looked over at Eli, who let out a long sigh.

"I heard he lost his farm. But I haven't seen him." Eli looked over at me. "He lost his farm to his brother. It's a whole thing."

"And what does that have to do with me getting the shit kicked out of me?" I asked, honestly confused.

"We're just looking into all possibilities."

Well, that was vague. But I had a feeling they weren't going to tell me anything else, and I wanted to get out of here. I answered a few more questions and they left, leaving me with more questions than answers.

"Okay, I'm going to get you back home and into your bed. And then we'll figure out more security for the distillery and bar," Ridge said.

"We need the open access on the west side," Eli said, before I could. "It leaves a vulnerable position for the rest of the property."

"We'll think of something."

"I hate being the problem child," I grumbled, the

pain coming back now that I wasn't distracted answering questions about the attack.

"You're not the problem child, you have a business that does good things for the family. We'll figure out a way to make it work," Eli offered. My cousin reached out and squeezed my shoulder, thankfully not the hurt one, before heading out.

"You can't work tomorrow, and now that Giselle is gone, what are you going to do?"

"I'm going to be fine," I grumbled. "And Giselle's been gone for a week. She was a shitty assistant manager anyway."

"Well, if you are down for the count, you want one of us to step in? Gabriel should be back soon," he said, speaking of our youngest brother.

"Gabriel's out on tour being the rockstar he is. I'm not going to have him behind the bar again; last time girls started screaming and wanting to know more about him than the actual drinks."

Ridge snorted. "Yeah, I guess he's losing his anonymity."

"I'll be fine. I can work tomorrow."

"You can't, but you've got family to rely on."

That was the reason I had moved here to start over. But I didn't like the idea that I had to lean on them. I didn't want to be the part of the family that fucked up. I didn't want to be the one that screwed over the Wilder legacy.

I didn't know what I was going to do, but I didn't think they were going to let me go back to work tomorrow, and Giselle, my former bartender and assistant manager, had left. She not only left us in a lurch, but she also hadn't been good at her job to begin with. I needed to hire someone. Someone who could handle the job and didn't bring drama.

But before I could find someone to replace her, I needed to get back to work.

As I got into Ridge's car and we made our way back to the property, I figured that at least one thing good happened tonight.

I was free.

No longer strapped to a problem that wouldn't go away.

I was free, and I was never going to be chained down again.

So why did that make me feel depressed as hell?

CHAPTER TWO

AVA

I didn't want to hate my job, but as hard as I tried, I couldn't help it. I had put myself into this situation, I was just going to have to deal with it. Sure, I probably should have finished college, and I probably should have picked a career other than being Aaron's wife, but there was no going back. Everything was fine.

If I kept telling myself that, I was totally going to believe it at some point.

It wasn't that I hated working. I had wanted to work full time and in a career of my choosing for all of my twenties. However, doing part-time jobs while married and raising Faith had been enough for me, because I'd had as much time with my daughter as possible.

I couldn't believe I had an eight-year-old. A loud, hyper, brilliant, and so full of energy eight-year-old. We were doing third grade math, third grade reading, and third grade everything. She was a bright spot in my life and was always in need of a hug because she was that much of a mama's girl.

And sometimes Faith cried herself to sleep at night because she missed her daddy.

While that cut at my heart with its sharp talons of self-hatred, I couldn't help but wonder exactly what she was missing, since Aaron hadn't truly been there for his daughter for longer than we had been divorced.

I hadn't realized what we could have had until I was able to step back and look at what I thought marriage was.

Having your husband cheat on you with one of your only adult friends, and then leaving you before you had a chance to break it off, just cemented the fact that I, Ava London, didn't have a great track record when it came to men, or good decisions.

Hence why, when I'd dropped out of college because I'd gotten pregnant with Faith, I'd had no backup plan.

Now I was working two jobs.

Today was the job I hated more than anything but gave me decent hours, *when* they had them. I stood in an old-fashioned diner, complete with plastic barstools, checkered mats, wearing a baby-blue dress uniform with a white starched apron and had to handwrite all my orders.

We were not living in an age where I had to hand-write anything or do tax math in our heads. Our boss had enough money to completely upgrade everything, but he liked the *experience*. Meaning our cook needed to be able to read my handwriting, and when he couldn't, he made up orders himself. He never asked for clarification, and he never let me explain, he said he knew best. And then I had to deal with the customers who didn't like their food, didn't like that they didn't get what they ordered, and then wouldn't tip me.

Oh yes, I *loved* my job.

But it was truly hard to find a job without references, education, or experience.

And my lovely ex-husband, when he'd left me and my daughter behind, had also taken everything else with him.

The TV, the furniture, and our savings accounts.

Including Faith's college fund.

He'd taken everything, and his high-priced lawyer, thanks to his parents, took the house, both cars, and left me with nothing. He had to pay child support, but he was always late with it. And the only way I could fight back was if I had money for a lawyer.

And I didn't.

Because the law didn't work the way you wanted. The law didn't always believe in you and work for you.

I had been so naive. Naive for trusting Aaron. Naive

trusting my own choices, and naive for trusting a system that never worked for me.

I was making do, getting by, and I hated myself for it.

"Ava, *attention*," my boss snapped out.

I was annoyed because I'd let my thoughts drift and had not only gotten caught by my boss, but buried myself in my own issues. I grinned, keeping a bright smile pasted on my face. "No problem, Bob. I'm on my way to table four."

"And skip to it or I'm putting you in the skates," he growled.

I resisted the urge to roll my eyes because the man would *never* put me in skates. There was no way he was going to risk hurting his precious linoleum floor. He buffed and babied that thing like no other. There was no way he was going to want scuff marks from skates, or my blood when I inevitably fell and broke something and bled everywhere.

No, I knew he was just testing me, and I was going to let him.

I needed this job.

Even though I hated where I worked, I hated smelling like syrup and eggs and pancakes and country fried chicken with gravy, as long as I worked weekend mornings, I got to have afternoons off every school day. Which meant I could pick up Ava and we could have mother-daughter time, while she worked on homework, and I worked on my online telemarketing business.

Together it somewhat all worked out, *if* I found a sitter for Saturdays and Sundays. It cut into my bottom line, but my neighbor in my rathole of an apartment complex watched my child. It was the scariest thing in the world trusting her, but so far it was working out.

"Hello there," I said to the table of four older men. "I'm Ava and I'll be taking care of you today. Can I get you some coffee or tea this morning?" I asked, keeping my voice chipper.

It wasn't the best job in the world, it wasn't even close to being fulfilling, but it put food on my table, and I got a free lunch every day I worked. That helped save money, and that lunch meant a lot because I didn't eat breakfast so I could make sure Faith got hers.

"I wouldn't mind a slice of you, hon," one of the older men who had to be pushing eighty said, as he leered at the too-tight fake cotton and polyester top straining against my breasts. I had to safety pin the buttons together because God forbid the owner Bob let me get a bigger size. No, he liked that my boobs were straining out of the top.

At this point I could probably go work at Twin Peaks and get more respect.

That wasn't out of the realm of possibility. While I knew I'd probably make more money, and there was nothing wrong with walking around in a low-cut top and tiny shorts, I didn't want to. I didn't want to *have* to.

But that wasn't what I was doing right now, so I just grinned at the older man.

"I think we're just serving coffee right now. But there is apple pie behind the case if you'd like that for breakfast."

The older man licked his lips as the guy next to him grunted and punched him in the arm.

"Sorry about Sam. He apparently needs caffeine in the morning, or he turns into a lech. We'll have four coffees, black, and your special. All over easy, white toast, no hash browns but fruit and cottage cheese on the side."

The other two men grunted in agreement and I took down the order, although I was pretty sure everybody who had seen these guys before knew their order by heart.

I grinned and made my way to the kitchen, putting the order on the rack and spinning it around.

"Order sent for table four," I called out.

"Got you, Ava," the cook grumbled.

He was always grumbling because he missed being able to smoke while on the job. Yes, it had been years since he had been able to, but it was his favorite thing.

So he complained about the lack of nicotine and I ignored him.

It was a good relationship. Mostly because there wasn't one.

"Ava," Bob snapped as I turned to him, steeling myself once again.

I wasn't sure what I had done wrong, but I had done something wrong. I was good at it according to him.

"Yes, Bob?"

"You didn't try to upsell anything. You didn't mention the specials, you didn't mention dessert or pancakes or anything. Or the fact that we have a gift card campaign going. You know the rules."

I smiled again, knowing that it didn't reach my eyes and I didn't give a flying fuck.

"They are regulars, according to Stacey," I said, speaking of the other waitress who had scurried off as soon as the table had gotten seated.

"And? Regulars can't change their mind? You know the rules. You have a quota."

Oh yes, the quota. The quota I reached eventually, but I was never the best. I hated trying to upsell things to people who clearly didn't want them. Yes, mentioning things so people could add it if they felt like it was one thing, being forced into asking if they wanted to smother and cover their hash browns even though they didn't even want hash browns to begin with wasn't my favorite thing.

"I'm sorry, I'll do better."

"You'd better. You're already on thin ice." He left then, and I let out a breath, turning to help Stacey with her large order.

"Sorry," Stacey whispered.

"You didn't do anything wrong," I said, the younger woman blushing.

She was in college, just trying to pay the bills, and had a bright future ahead of her.

I on the other hand wasn't sure what the future would be for me.

I just needed to tough this out until I found something else that could work.

Because this was for Faith.

It wasn't like I could go and move in with my mother. She had moved to Canada to be with her new husband. And while my mother was finally thriving, finally happy after so many years of mourning my father, it wasn't easy to move in with her. There was the whole not being a citizen thing, and visas, and everything that came with over-the-border moves.

And the fact that my mom didn't know how bad it was? Well, I wasn't going to think about that too hard.

I helped Stacey with the next order, and then I

worked on the next table, getting Sam and his little friends their orders out as well.

Everything became rote, and I wondered how long I could handle this.

I needed to find a better job. But doing what I had done in college, bartending, wasn't great when you had a young daughter at home. While working nights meant I would have the days with my daughter, no one would be there to watch her while she slept. And I couldn't spend all my money on childcare.

There didn't seem to be a solution, and once again I hated Aaron for what he had done.

He had taken everything from us, our money, our home, and my dignity.

And he had taken whatever love he had pretended to have for his child.

That I wouldn't forgive him for. All of that and the dignity part. But it wasn't like I had any of that left to care about.

Another man came in, this time alone, and sat in one of my two-top booths. The hostess fluffed her hair a bit as she walked by him, and I rolled my eyes.

Well, it seemed that a hot guy had just sat in my section. I didn't care because there was no way I was ever dating again.

No thank you.

I grabbed my notepad and made my way over.

"Hello there, I'm Ava. I'll be taking care of you." The fake smile I had plastered over my face faltered as soon as I saw who it was.

Wyatt Wilder looked up at me, a brow raised, the surprise on his face evident.

Well, hell.

This wasn't one of the two people that I never wanted to see again in my life, but he was top five. Not because I hated him. Not really. Okay, maybe a little.

Because Wyatt Wilder was a *Nice Guy*. Trademark and everything. He also happened to be Aaron's former best friend, and Wyatt's ex-wife had been my friend— the one about to marry Aaron.

It was a twisted web of complications that I wanted nothing more to do with.

I had dated and married the nice guy, who turned out to be a complete asshole. Wyatt reminded me so much of him that we had never gotten along.

"Ava?" Wyatt asked. "What are you doing here?"

I swallowed hard, ignoring the red blush stealing up my neck. I would not be embarrassed or ashamed for working here. I had to provide for my daughter.

Fuck this man for thinking that he was too good for this place.

Of course, he hadn't said anything like that, but I could feel the derision from him.

There was little Ava, working at a shitty diner

because she didn't have anything else, while he and his family ran the gamut at the beautiful Wilder Retreat. Oh, I had heard about it, even though we hadn't lived here long. You couldn't escape the Wilders.

"Hello there, Wyatt. What can I get you to drink?"

"I didn't even realize you lived this close. Seriously, here?" he asked, and this time the derision wasn't hidden at all.

"A woman's got to work. And there's nothing wrong with working. Hard work helps save lives."

"I know that, it's just, well..." his voice trailed off. "I'll take coffee. Sugar and cream. But not too much? Hell, I think I've forgotten how to order."

"It's fine. I've got you. You need more time with the menu?"

I went over the specials, and he shook his head. "I'll just do an egg white omelet and fruit."

"Going heart-healthy?"

Wyatt snorted. "No, I just had a long night, and grease doesn't really sound too good for me." He shifted in his seat, and that's when I realized that he had dark circles under his eyes and looked to be stiff and in pain.

I wanted to ask him what happened, but Wyatt was not my friend.

And with my boss breathing down my neck, I didn't have time to stand here for too long.

I took his order and as I was turning away from the drop-off point for my order, I nearly dropped everything.

"Faith?" I asked, my babysitter coming forward with my daughter trailing behind her.

"Mom!" Faith called out as she ran to me. I held out my arms and she slammed into me, her arms coming around my waist.

I could pick her up if I wanted to, even though my baby girl was getting so tall and grown up now, but my boss was watching, and I could also feel Wyatt's eyes on me.

Oh why did he have to be here?

"What's wrong? Hello, baby," I said, running my hand down my daughter's hair.

"I need to go. Johnny got a job out in Houston, and it's going to be a couple of weeks. So I need to head out now. I figured she can sit here and color or something?"

I blinked at Francie, my neighbor and babysitter. Her boyfriend was a musician who was in a really shitty band, and I could hear their music through the thin bedroom walls, just like I could hear whenever they had bad sex. My daughter's room was on the other side of the living room, so thankfully she couldn't hear any of that. But still, this couldn't have come at a worse time.

"Francie, are you serious?" I asked, the bottom

falling out of my stomach as the reality of her words and my upcoming dire situation settled in.

"I'm sorry. I just have a lot of things to do. And this could be a big thing for Johnny." *I doubted it.* "Anyway, I've been cutting you a break."

People were staring now, mortification settling in. I did not have a backup plan for this weekend. I did not have anyone to watch my daughter.

And with Bob storming over here, I knew I wasn't going to have another way out. "Please, Francie. Just for today," I begged.

I would get down on my knees on this fake tile floor and beg to keep my kid safe and fed. I'd do *anything* for Faith. And I'd find a way to fix this tomorrow. I had to.

"I'm sorry. I've got to go. Bye, Faith!" Francie said as she waved and skipped out, as if she wasn't ruining my life. Because every time somebody left, they found a way to bring me down with them.

I couldn't fault Francie. I mean I could, because this was ridiculous, but I couldn't truly hate her for it because she had been doing me a favor. And now I wasn't sure what I was supposed to do.

"Mommy? What's wrong?" Faith asked, and I kept running my hand down her hair, trying to figure out how to fix this.

I didn't have a backup plan. I didn't have a way to make this work.

Oh, God. I was totally and utterly screwed.

"Ava?" Bob said. "You know the rules. No personal time at work. Your daughter can't stay here. I don't take freeloaders."

I winced at his tone and turned to him. "I just need one minute to figure this out and I'll be right back to work."

"You're not on break. You don't get that minute."

"Bob, just one minute." I swallowed hard. "Please."

"One minute is not going to fix this. You know the rules."

"Ava?" Wyatt asked.

"Wyatt, I got this."

"Wyatt?" Faith asked, as she ran to him, throwing her arms around him.

I ignored the sinking feeling in my gut as Wyatt picked her up and put her on his hip, as if she was still the two-year-old he had once known.

"Hello there, Faith darling." He looked up at me, that damn strong jaw of his working as he put two and two together about this current predicament. "I didn't know you worked here. I was just here getting breakfast. It's good to see you."

"Ava," Bob growled.

"Here, Faith can join me for breakfast." There was no way I was going to allow that to happen, and I tried to say something, but Faith just clung to Wyatt.

And that's when I realized that Faith, my daughter, hadn't seen Wyatt in far too long. He had always been good to my daughter. Even when we hadn't gotten along, he had always been kind to her.

And I didn't have another backup plan. I didn't have a backup plan to begin with.

I was a terrible mother. A terrible mother who really needed this job.

"Ava, come here," Bob snapped. "If you're going to keep taking personal time, you can take it right outside that door."

"I'm sorry, Wyatt, thank you," I blurted, not having another answer.

I turned, and ran right into Jeff, another one of our servers.

And his order of seven plates on one tray, fell to the ground, the sound of shattering ceramic echoing through the diner. Sunny-side-up eggs smeared on the floor, the toast and sausage links rolled away, and as Bob's face turned red, and Jeff started moaning in fear, I stood there frozen, wondering if I could just redo today. Wondering if there was anything I could have done better.

"You're fired," Bob snapped. "Get out of here. And don't come back unless it's for your final check." He kept yelling, but I couldn't focus on the words, not with the world crashing down around me and my heart a staccato drumbeat in my ear.

Dozens of eyes bored into me as the tableau became the center of everyone's attention, and I could not believe that my daughter and Wyatt were witnessing this.

Desperation clung to me, and I wanted to beg for my job, but I wouldn't. I had begged before, begged for Aaron to keep his word and not break my daughter's heart, but there was nothing else.

I kept my chin high, that pride of mine the only thing I had left even though it was a facade and grabbed my purse from under the counter.

"Fine. Fine," I muttered, and went to Wyatt and Faith.

"Thank you for holding her."

"Ava," Wyatt whispered, and I shook my head before taking my daughter, setting her on her feet, and walking out of the building.

I had no idea what I was going to do. My other part-time job did not pay enough, and I knew I was going to have to go get a job bartending. But I needed a babysitter for that.

There were just no options. Christmas was coming and while Faith was out of school for now thanks to a longer than average break, her classes would start up soon and she'd end up going to a campus I hated for her.

Tears were threatening, and so was panic, but I couldn't do that. I couldn't afford to do that.

The door opened behind me, and I hoped that it was maybe Sam trying to hit on me. Maybe I could marry an eighty-year-old man and call it a day. That would be so much better.

But it wasn't him.

Of course it wasn't.

"Ava, I'm sorry."

I turned to Wyatt, keeping a fake bright smile on my face because my daughter needed to see it.

"It's okay. This job wasn't great for us anyway. We're going to go find something else, aren't we?" I asked, but Faith was eight years old now and she didn't believe my lies any more than I did.

Her eyes started to fill, and I held out my arm so she could lean into me.

"It's okay, baby. We'll figure it out," I whispered, not having any idea how I was going to figure it out.

"I'm looking for an assistant manager and bartender at the distillery," Wyatt blurted.

I froze and stared at him, wondering why the hell he was still here.

He continued as if I didn't look like a guppy lost in a vast ocean with a shark on my tail. "I know it's probably not ideal, but we have a place to stay on the property too, so you can have someone to watch Faith there. We have childcare and everything. It's not much, but hell, Ava." He winced. "Sorry for cursing, but seriously. Let me help, like I should have done to begin with."

Faith kept hold of me, but I felt her turn her head towards Wyatt. I didn't want to say yes.

I didn't want it to be him who offered to help me.

Why did it have to be him?

"I...Wyatt."

"Let me help. *For Faith*," he reiterated, and I swallowed hard.

I didn't have anything to say, as there were no words left. Just an unending agony of my own poor choices and failures.

"For Faith." I cleared my throat, my hands shaking. "Okay. I don't know about the assistant manager thing, but I can bartend." And working for the Wilders would be safer than working some places. That much I knew. They took care of their people.

He nodded and looked down at Faith. "Well, since I'm never eating there again, I'm going to go find someplace else to eat, probably on my own property like I should have. You know where it is?"

I nodded, feeling awkward and out of place and so lost that I didn't know what to say. Though that lost feeling should be familiar at this point. After all, it's what my life had turned into.

"Wyatt..."

He shook his head. "Let me help. We'll figure it out. I need the help. Seriously."

I looked at the dark circles under his eyes, the way he was holding himself, and I knew he had a story to tell. But not to me, and not in front of my daughter.

I nodded and knew this could only be temporary. But I didn't have another choice.

Faith deserved so much better. We both did. But for some reason I didn't think of me, only my daughter.

Faith immediately went to Wyatt and hugged him, and he didn't resist a single moment before hugging her back. Tears threatened again but I ignored them. Just like I ignored everything else about what I was feeling.

Because Faith was first. Always. Even if this moment took every last ounce of pride I thought I'd had left.

CHAPTER THREE
AVA

As I closed the trunk on my aging fifth-hand SUV, I prayed that the latch wouldn't pop open on the highway. The slightly crooked off-red SUV and the small U-Haul trailer attached to my hitch were filled with nearly all my worldly possessions.

I took a step back, my throat threatening to seize as I took in all before me.

This was it.

Everything that I owned—no furniture, just clothes and a few memories. Whatever memories I was allowed to keep that is, and my daughter in the backseat looking at me through the closed window.

I gave her a brave smile. She waved back, excited for the new adventure.

That much at least was true. Faith loved Uncle

Wyatt, a man she hadn't seen for a year until that chance meeting in the diner, and couldn't wait to hang out with him some more. Faith was grateful to get out of this apartment, just as much as I was. I just didn't realize it was all going to be happening at once.

Aaron had taken so much, but I had let him tell me I was the one who was the trouble. I was the one who kept making the mistakes. Aaron did it purposely; I did it by my own wrong decisions, and so who was the villain in this situation?

Was it Bob, who had fired me without real cause? He had always hated me, probably because I hadn't wanted to sleep with him the first afternoon that I worked there. Or maybe he just didn't like his life.

And since I had been fired, and then hired by someone I never expected to see again, everything had turned topsy-turvy. I had come back to my apartment that was on a six-month lease, with a note stapled to my door.

Not an eviction notice, but a warning. There was going to be new management, and everybody's leases weren't going to be re-upped in three weeks like we all planned. Francie wouldn't be happy once she came back to see that. *If* she came back.

Bile filled my mouth again as I remembered that feeling.

Homeless. Jobless. And a single mom.

This was not what I expected for my life.

But I was stronger than this. I had to be.

I didn't have a choice.

Faith needed me. And I needed her.

The back door opened, and Faith stuck her head out. "Are you ready to go, Mommy?"

I smiled over at her. "You know it. It's a twenty-minute drive. Do you need to go to the bathroom before we leave?"

She shook her head. "Nope. I'm okay. I can't wait to see the ranch."

I steeled myself because we were going into parts unknown. I hadn't really thought about Wyatt's offer of having a place to stay for Faith when I worked evenings. I had just needed to get out of the parking lot of that diner, to strip off my too-starched uniform. I swore I could still smell the syrup in my hair even though I had showered one last time in my too-small, too-rickety shower.

But as soon as I had seen the note, I hadn't had time to dwell, to wallow. I bucked up and called Wyatt right away.

He had answered on the first ring. "Ava? You backing out?" I was silent for so long, that he cursed on the other line. "I'm sorry. Do you need some help?"

"That place that you said we could stay for late nights at work—what about days?" I'd tried to keep my voice strong and yet I heard the fear woven through the tone.

Wyatt was silent for so long this time that I was afraid I had said something wrong. I was on my last cord, my last chance. And I didn't know what to do.

Asking for help was not my favorite thing in the world, something I was still learning how to do, but I needed to.

"Do you want me to come pick you up? Where are you?"

I shook my head even though he couldn't see me. "I'm renting a U-Haul; I don't have much." Wyatt had cursed because he knew who had taken everything. I didn't know the ins and outs of his divorce with Isabelle, but he had clearly come out a little bit better than I had. We both moved to this area, me because it had been the only place I could afford, him because he had family here.

"I just need a place to stay for a little while. Until I get my feet back under me."

"It's yours. For as long as you want it." He had paused. "And it's not a shared house or anything. I'm close by if you need anything, but it's also close to a lot of my siblings. And cousins. So it's not, well, it's going to be weird."

I had laughed at that. "I don't believe you on that. At least the weird part."

Wyatt joined in with his deep chuckle. "You're right. Do you need help lifting anything?"

"There's not that much, sadly."

"Ava." I didn't know what that tone meant, so I ignored it. I couldn't take his pity. Not right then. I'd do anything for Faith, but I was nearing my breaking point.

"Can you just text me the directions again?" I had asked while I stood in my apartment, knowing I had only a few hours to pack.

"Of course. Then we'll talk about the job thing. You don't have to do this alone, Ava."

I had sighed at that, knowing how wrong he was. "I just need Faith to be in a safe place to sleep tonight. Then I'll figure it out."

"That much I can do. For Faith," he had repeated.

And my world had changed.

Now here I was, after dropping off the keys to an apartment that I hadn't wanted but had needed, in a car filled with too many memories and yet not enough, on our way to the Wilders.

"It's not a ranch," I repeated to Faith, who didn't believe me.

"He doesn't have horses?"

I shook my head. "Not that I know of. I know there's a garden for the restaurants. And maybe a goat or two, and some chickens."

"That's a ranch!" She sounded so happy again, so I

left it at that. She was so damn resilient, and I reminded myself to be the same.

"Maybe more of a farm."

"What's the difference?"

I opened my mouth to say, then realized I didn't know. I'm sure they mentioned it in middle school or something, but I couldn't remember. "I think a ranch is more animals and farms are more crops. Why don't we look that up later?"

"Okay."

My baby was freaking adorable, and conversations with her always brought that smile to my face. "And it's the Wilder Retreat and Winery."

"Like wine for adults?"

"Yep. It's good wine too." Wilder Wines were one of my favorites, not that I had ever told Wyatt that. To be honest, I hadn't known it was in his family's holdings until after the divorce. The fact that his cousins owned and operated it, and now Wyatt oversaw the Wilder Distillery and vodka branch, was shocking to me. Not shocking that Wyatt was doing well. It was just the fact that he was doing so much better than he had when he was married.

"And you said they have weddings there?" Faith asked as I got off the highway.

"Yes. Weddings and parties and other things. It's a huge place that I've heard good things about."

"And we're going to live there?"

"Just for a little bit, until we figure out what to do next. And Wyatt got me a job so I can be close to you."

"But what about school?" Faith asked, and I pressed my lips together. We were just hitting winter break, and I hated my daughter's school. It was overfilled, with too many students per teacher, and so much homework. Faith hadn't made a single friend there, and it hurt both of us to think about it. However, I had a plan.

Mostly thanks to Wyatt.

Another reason I had to hate the man. I resented needing help.

"There's a school nearby that a lot of people who have children that work on the property go to. And I've already contacted them thanks to one of Wyatt's family members, so we're going to be all set."

"I hope it's better than the other one. Not that I didn't like Ms. Johnson, but sometimes she was mean."

My hands gripped the steering wheel hard as I tried to think of something to say. I didn't like Ms. Johnson. She had been rude and outright cruel to my daughter. She had judged us for where we lived and that I was a single mom. It didn't matter that there were other single parents there, we were new to the area, therefore we were unwanted.

"Well, we're going to try this new adventure."

"And I'm going to stay here for the whole rest of the

year?" Faith asked, her voice low.

I was a horrible mother. A completely horrible mother.

"Yes. The whole year."

Even if I had to live in a tent to make that happen, my daughter was going to finish out this school year here. I still hadn't talked to her new teacher, but Wyatt's cousin-in-law Alexis was already working things out. I didn't even know the woman, and she was helping us.

It didn't make any sense, but we were making do. I had to learn how to rely on people because doing it myself was not working.

"And Dad will find us?" Faith asked, her voice so soft, as if she were afraid to hurt me, or maybe even herself.

I took another turn down a farm road, trying to keep my attention on my surroundings and my daughter at the same time.

"I left him a message. He'll know exactly where you are."

Not that he would ever come to visit or call, but I didn't say that.

"Do I get to pet the chickens?" Faith asked and my lips twitched, grateful that she was changing the subject.

As we continued to discuss the merits of chickens

and goats, I looked around the hills of the San Antonio area.

The hill country of South Texas really wasn't mountainous, but there were still hills. And it was gorgeous, even in winter. Around this time in South Texas some of the trees were just now turning colors, while the rest of them were either green or had lost their leaves altogether. The fields were all brown and yellow, but it worked with the aesthetic. The Wilders lived in what Wyatt had jokingly called a compound right outside San Antonio and on the way to the New Braunfels area. It was sort of like Fredericksburg in terms of wineries and breweries, but a little more east. When it was greener, I knew it had to be gorgeous. There were still suburban neighborhoods that we drove by, pop-up places that had come with new developments, as well as old ranch houses that seemed to be huge mansions. We drove by longhorns and horses. And some goats.

It was somehow farmland and suburbia all rolled into one, halfway between San Antonio and Austin. I knew one day as urban development continued to crawl it would all be one big city, with New Braunfels somehow in the middle.

But right now, I had to focus on the present, and not whatever the hell was coming next.

I wasn't sure of the layout of the retreat, and I needed to look on the map to see what each of the buildings were, but I hadn't had time. There was a spa and a few cabins, a huge inn, a welcome center, a wedding venue, as well as the winery, vines, distillery, and the restaurants. The Wilders were making a name for themselves.

They were making it work.

Which worked for me.

At least for now.

"Wow," Faith said from the backseat, and I agreed with her sentiment as we came up over the hill and saw the beautiful old white-and-gray buildings that had to be the Wilder Retreat.

It was truly elegant and sprawling. There were cedar and oak trees everywhere, but you could still see the gorgeous buildings popping up all over the area.

Everything was fenced off as well, and I knew they did that for security, and considering who had married into the Wilders it made sense, so all I could do was follow the GPS and make my way to the front gates.

There was a security guard in the front office, and I rolled down my window as we got there.

It made me a little nervous that they had all this security; how high-end was this place? I thought of my beat-up SUV and my U-Haul and wondered if they were going to tell us to go around back with the staff or something. After all, we were staff.

"Hello, welcome to the Wilder Retreat and Winery.

Are you here to check in?" the kind man asked.

I swallowed hard. "No, I'm Ava, Ava London? I'm here to see Wyatt."

The man smiled and didn't even bother to look down at his notes. "Hello, Ava, and you must be Faith," the man said as he waved behind me.

"Hi!" Faith called back.

I was surprised and a little off-kilter. "Oh. So he told you we were coming?"

"He did. You are going to want to head left at the main juncture towards the distillery, and he'll meet you out there to show you where to unload everything. You're more than welcome to head to the main building afterwards to meet everybody, but this way you can get all settled."

And this way I wouldn't have to park my monstrosity of a vehicle in front of the gorgeous multi-million-dollar mansion. That made sense.

Maybe I needed to stop being so bitter. After all, I knew Wyatt hadn't grown up like this. But there was still resentment because all I could think about was Aaron.

Damn that man.

Or at least damn me.

"Oh. Thank you," I said, trying to calm my nerves.

"No problem. Welcome to the Wilders, Ava and Faith. We're happy to have you here."

The man smiled at me as the huge wrought iron gates opened. I swallowed hard, wondering exactly what I had just gotten myself into.

We drove up the winding path, past the main house and the signs for the spa and winery, and took a left where he told us, towards the distillery.

"It's beautiful. We're going to live here?" Faith asked in awe.

I pressed my lips together, trying not to hyperventilate. This was so out of my wheelhouse. "For a little while, yes. Until we get our feet back under us." Because I did not want to lie to my daughter more than I already had to when it came to her father.

"This is going to be fun! Now I'm not so worried about school because I'm going to have friends here, I know it."

I winced, trying to hold back my nerves. "We are going to find you friends. I promise."

"And you too?"

"And me too," I whispered.

"Aunt Rory's here too, right?"

I smiled at that, thinking of my childhood friend who had just moved back to the area. "Yes. She's on a work trip right now but when she gets back, she's going to learn all about our new adventures."

"Yay!"

Oh yes, Rory was going to have a lot to say about

what had just happened.

I should have called her, but I was embarrassed. And it wasn't like she had room for us anyway. She had a small apartment, and though I knew if I needed to we could have crashed at her place, I wasn't going to inconvenience her. I was just going to inconvenience Wyatt.

As I pulled up to the distillery, a woman in a gorgeous dress covering her baby bump came out, followed by another woman with long dark hair piled up on her head.

They both were gorgeous, and I pressed my lips together, smiling back as they waved.

Oh hell.

When I parked, both women came up to the car, and I got out.

"Ava? I'm Alexis. We talked on the phone?"

Relieved that I recognized her voice, I nodded. "Yes, that's me. Let me just get Faith out."

"I've got it, Mommy," Faith said, as she jumped out of the car.

When she did things like that, it reminded me that she wasn't a baby girl anymore. Oh, she was still my little girl, but she was getting bigger and bigger every day.

"I'm Aurora, I'm with Wyatt's brother Ridge," the other woman said.

"Oh, and I'm married to Wyatt's cousin Eli," Alexis

added.

I nodded, trying to keep up with everyone's names but knew I wasn't going to. It didn't help that Wyatt's seven cousins all had names that started with the letter E. Their parents had been insane when they had done that.

"It's nice to meet you guys. Thank you for meeting me here, though I thought I was meeting Wyatt."

Aurora winced. "He had a doctor's appointment that he couldn't get out of."

"In other words, we forced him into actually keeping it so he can get his ribs checked out rather than pushing it aside."

I leaned forward in alarm as Faith took my hand.

"Is Uncle Wyatt, okay?"

Both women smiled brightly, but I saw the worry in their gazes.

"Oh yes, he is. He should be coming back soon. He just needed his checkup."

"I don't like checkups. I always get shots," Faith grumbled.

I grinned at that. "Don't worry, I've got your back," I said, squeezing my daughter's hand.

"Maybe. But I still have to get shots," she grumbled sweetly.

"Anyway, we're going to hop into our car, and you can follow us down to the cabin you'll be staying at."

I blinked. "Cabin?" I asked.

"Oh, you're going to love it. I stayed there when I visited here for the first time. It's perfect for the two of you, and when you're working, Faith is going to come hang out with us in the main building," Aurora put in.

"Oh. Right." I cleared my throat. "I guess we should go over all that."

Alexis nodded. "I know we went over everything in email, but we'll review it. And I know Wyatt's going to want to talk to you later about hours and everything. But let's get you all settled first. I know after a long drive and having to pack up everything, you must be exhausted."

I ran my hands through my hair. "Does it look it?"

"Not in the slightest, but we've all been there," Alexis said pointedly, and from the way she looked at me, I had a feeling maybe she had. Everybody came with baggage and memories. It wasn't just me. I had to remember that.

"Are you having a baby?" Faith asked and I winced, squeezing my daughter's hand.

"Faith, you remember we said not to ask questions like that." Things could get awkward.

Alexis grinned. "I am. This is my second one."

"So you have another baby? Can they be my friend?" she asked quickly, and my heart ached.

"Of course. Kylie's five-and-a-half, so you're a little

older than her, but she loves everyone."

"And there's two twins on the property too, Reese and Cassie, they're six, but they play with everyone," Aurora added.

"See? Look at all the fun friends you're going to make."

"I don't care if they're younger. I can teach them everything that I know."

"That may be a little worrisome," I said deadpan as Faith laughed, and suddenly I felt a little more at ease.

This wasn't perfect, but it was something.

It wasn't a diner where I felt uncomfortable and unwanted. With just a few short words, these women were ready to bring tears to my eyes with how welcoming they were.

I didn't want to have to rely on Wyatt. I didn't want to have to rely on someone who reminded me so much of Aaron. So much of everything we lost.

I needed help. And though I resented it, I was going to do this for Faith. We were going to formulate a plan. And when it all fell out from under me once again, we would land on our feet and move on. Just like we kept doing.

I had to hope I wasn't harming my daughter in the process.

But I was relying on Wyatt. And I knew I had to be grateful, even though I never felt more lost in my life.

CHAPTER FOUR

WYATT

"So how are the ribs?"

I instinctively put my hand over my side and frowned at my brother's words. "They're fine."

Not quite a lie, though not quite the truth. In fact, if I took a deep breath it felt like somebody was trying to crush my ribs with their fists. But they weren't broken, only bruised. Although considering the treatment for either seemed to be the exact same fucking thing, I wasn't sure if that was better or not.

"So, you're lying to me?" Brooks asked as he handed over a cup of coffee. We stood in his kitchen, and I was just grateful I didn't have to make the coffee myself. When I took a sip, I smiled at the fact that he had gotten my coffee and cream and sugar ratio correct.

"Tasty."

"I might as well just put an entire piece of cake in that cup with the amount of sugar that you like."

"It's fake sugar at least. You know, the kind that isn't that bad for you." I took another sip, embracing the fact that I was not a black coffee guy. I didn't have to be. I was allowed to enjoy my sweet concoction.

"It's going to rot your teeth."

"I've had one cavity in my life," I said as I knocked on wood. "And that was because of my braces."

"Sure, blame the braces."

"I can and I will. Seriously, it's just brushing and flossing your teeth. And having damn good genetics." I grinned my pearly whites and my brother just rolled his eyes.

"Plus, I feel like black coffee is worse for your enamel than the sugar. If anything, I'm blocking my enamel from the black coffee and therefore helping reduce staining."

Brooks blinked at me. "I believe none of what you just said is true. In fact, the rationalizations that you're using might be so poorly done that they are almost believable."

I lifted my cup in his direction. "You are welcome. My delusions really get me through the day. It's how I function on so little sleep, considering we must have a lovely Wilder meeting in the mornings, even though I work fucking nights."

Brooks rolled his eyes. "Oh, is the little baby crying and tired?"

"Fuck you," I grumbled.

"I'm so glad to hear that you guys are getting along," Ridge joked as he walked in and went directly to the coffee maker.

"Don't you and your woman have your own coffee?" Brooks grumbled, although there was no heat in it. Brooks always tended to act like the eldest brother even though he wasn't. That title went to Ridge, who also acted like the oldest brother.

Gabriel and I were the youngest, Gabe being the baby of the family. Which was something I liked to rub in his face often. It didn't matter that we were nearing thirty, that was just how life went. How my parents dealt with four boys, I'll never know.

At least they didn't have to deal with six boys and a girl, like my aunt and uncle had. I still wasn't quite sure how they had ever made it through adolescence and the teenage years.

"I want my second cup. I'm running late."

From the cat-in-cream look on Ridge's face, I had a feeling I knew why he was running late.

"Poor Aurora. Never allowed to get any sleep," I teased.

He flipped me off. "She is at work. Somebody must bake and decorate all the cakes for this wedding venue."

"Is she trying that caramel crunch cake today?" I asked, my mouth watering.

"You and your fucking sweet tooth," Brooks said with a laugh as he took a sip of his black coffee. Brooks liked both black coffee and coffee with sugar and cream, he mixed it up. The fact that he was teasing me meant he was trying to get his mind off the fact that I had been hurt. It was what we did—acted fucking ridiculous.

"Any idea what this meeting is about?" Brooks asked after a moment, and I winced.

"Probably because I hired a new assistant manager and bartender without asking or doing any background checks."

Ridge pointed at me. "Got it in one."

"Ava's good, though. She's good people."

"Then why did you always hate her?" Brooks asked.

Ridge leaned forward. "Wait, he hates her? What did I miss?"

I sighed, knowing that keeping the connection secret wouldn't do anyone any good. "Ava is Aaron's ex-wife."

"That much I knew, but you two didn't, like, get it on in retaliation or anything, did you?" Ridge asked. Without looking, I threw the orange on the counter at him. Ridge caught it and shrugged. "I'm hungry anyway and could use the vitamin C. But how about I say that in a non-dumbass way. So you and Ava never..."

I shook my head. "No. We were just friends." I paused. "Okay, I was friends with Aaron. She was friends with Isabelle. And then, well, you know. Life."

"I don't know anything," Ridge clapped back, his brows raised.

My brothers were great at getting under my skin, though Ava was always worse. Odd to think that since I tried not to think of her. Or at least, hadn't thought of her at all. "Fine, we always got under each other's skin. Probably because we're so much alike."

"Well, that's an astute observation," Brooks added, drinking his coffee.

"I don't know, we just were similar in some aspects, and then different in others. Plus, she had to deal with Aaron all day. That would make anybody growly."

Brooks sighed. "I thought he was your friend."

"I thought he was, too," I said.

Ridge shook his head. "So you hired Ava. And I've already done a background check. That guy did a number on her."

My eyes widened. "Are you fucking serious? I knew she had to be working at that diner for a reason and needed a place to stay, but what the hell. I don't know everything about her divorce. I haven't really talked to her since the whole thing blew up."

As in, when I had walked in on my former best friend and ex-wife having sex in our bed. Later that afternoon I had seen Ava and Aaron yelling at each other by his truck, but I hadn't seen her again. I hadn't seen Faith either. That little girl had grown up so much since then. However, even though she had run to me and hugged me, she had been a little more fearful. What the hell had that man done to his family?

"I can't tell you all the information because it's privileged," Ridge answered.

He had to be kidding. "I'm her boss. I should know these things."

"Maybe. Or maybe you should talk to her."

Feeling a setup, I narrowed my eyes. "Are you serious?"

"Your former best friend is an asshole. There's a reason she needs the job, a reason she doesn't have a place. The reason that little girl doesn't have a college fund."

"I'm going to fucking kill him." I fisted my hands in front of me, my heart racing. Aaron deserved a lot more than the punch he'd gotten to the face when he'd come at me that day when he'd told me that Isabelle was his. At that point, I hadn't even been fighting for my wife— which was a testament in itself. No, I'd been fighting my best friend for lying and betraying me.

And he'd done it all to Ava as well...and much worse, it seemed.

"He had a better lawyer than her. I'm pretty sure he had a better lawyer than you." Ridge shook his head. "She got full custody, though. That's why she was able to switch schools and Alexis could help so easily."

"I hadn't even thought about shit like that. I just wanted to help them. I blame the concussion."

"You didn't have a concussion," Brooks corrected.

"Just let me have my own delusions. So, we really must hold a whole meeting about who I hired?" I asked. "Because seriously, I was going to hire someone anyway."

"She doesn't have managerial experience," Ridge put in.

"You want me to fire her and put her and her kid on the streets?"

"I'm not saying that. And it's just a normal meeting. If you think Ava can handle it? Go for it. Can't be any worse than your last person."

I snorted. "Pretty much. But she was a good bartender, and organized every single trip that we took as two couples. And, well, I didn't want to see Faith on the streets. Sue me."

"You're a good man, Wyatt Wilder," Ridge said softly, and I flipped him off just because I could.

"I don't want to go to this meeting."

"Suck it up."

"You know, I find it highly suspicious that Gabriel doesn't have to join us for these meetings even though he owns a stake in it."

"He owns a stake in it because he was the one to help us with the down payments so we could buy in with the cousins," Ridge corrected. "Cousin Eliza doesn't have a stake anymore either, but she still sometimes video chats her way into the events."

"Eliza lives in Colorado; she has an excuse."

"And Gabriel is out touring the country, and soon the world. You know the Grammys are coming soon."

"Isn't Lark nominated too?" I asked about our cousin's wife.

"Yep. Big time all around for the Wilders. New hires, Grammys, babies coming. Weddings. You know, everything."

I grinned. "You and Aurora setting the date soon?"

Ridge just sipped his coffee. "Eventually. Though I think she wants to bake her own cake."

"Because that's not going to add to the stress at all," Brooks said.

I looked over at my brother again, wondering if he was okay working at a place that had so many weddings and memories. Then again, Ridge was dealing with it too. We all were.

Ridge had lost his fiancée, I had divorced the one

woman I thought I loved, and Brooks, well, Brooks had gone through a hell of his own.

Gabriel was the only one unscathed when it came to relationships, as far as I knew. Of course, our baby brother would have to talk about it for us to know.

"Come on, let's head to the meeting and I can get more coffee."

"You know that much coffee is not good for you," I teased my older brother.

"I was up all night, and very early this morning. I'm going to need coffee."

"Bragger," Brooks joked and I laughed, still slightly sore.

Today was going to be Ava's first day, so yes, a meeting was in store, and I hoped that I wasn't doing the wrong thing.

But keeping Faith safe? That didn't seem like the wrong thing.

Though I kept asking myself why I had to constantly rationalize that I was doing this for Faith and not for her mother, who used to be my friend.

But maybe some questions were better left unanswered.

BY THE TIME I GOT TO THE BAR AND DISTILLERY —my distillery manager was already working full time during the day—I was ready to set up for the bar service. We were open for lunch and dinner, and then into the late nights. We had different closing hours weekends and according to the laws set by the state. The distillery was a separate business, and we had hired good people for it. I was not a chemist or any form of scientist. But I knew what kind of liquor I liked. So I had taken classes, learned who to hire, and learned how to manage it all. The Wilder vodka line was going strong, with more variations to come. I liked having a Texas-based liquor that we could get into stores, and maybe one day go nationwide. Just like Wilder wines was doing.

Apparently, the Wilders were trying to take over the world. My cousins had wanted a stake in the liquor distribution of the area, and I had helped, but I didn't run it. My manager Sam did.

And I was damn fine with that because running a bar and grill was enough work.

Sam didn't need my help thankfully, so I went behind the bar to go see what I needed to fix. In the few days since the attack, Brooks along with East, my cousin, had already cleaned up everything and fixed the broken handles.

I should be bothered that everything was cleaned up

so quickly and easily, but I wasn't. We hadn't found the money bag, but thankfully the guy hadn't gotten the larger one. Security tapes didn't catch his face, although they had been running. That meant Ridge and Trace had added even more security. We didn't have a bouncer, nor did I think we needed one, but if Ridge felt that we did, I would take it. I didn't want to get beat up again. And now that I was going to have Ava here at night running the place alone with the staff, maybe we did need one.

Dread curled in my gut. Hiring her was a mistake. Not because it was Ava, but because it was *Ava*.

That didn't make any sense at all.

"Wyatt?"

I turned to see Ava walking towards me, her eyes looking a little wary.

"Hey. You're here right on time." I looked down at my watch. "Okay, a little early."

Her lips twitched. "I was nervous, wanted to make sure I didn't miss the place."

"Kind of hard when we're all on the same compound, right?"

"Maybe. It does feel a little commune-esque."

I rolled my eyes. "We're all businesses. Eli's not the commune leader." I postured. "That I know of. I am newer to the area than the rest of them."

Her lips twitched and her shoulders relaxed.

"Well, that's good to know. So, today's my first day?"

"Yep. I know you know how to bartend, but let's go over how to be an assistant manager."

"Wyatt, I don't have any experience."

I shrugged. "I didn't either. I learned. So let's do this."

"I hate that this feels like charity."

"It's not. You're going to be working hard, believe me. Or at least I hope you'll be working harder than my last person."

"You know I work hard. It still feels like charity. Even though I need it."

"Aaron's an asshole."

Her eyes flared. "So you know?"

I winced, feeling bad that Ridge had mentioned anything. "Some. You don't have to tell me." I let out a breath. "It just makes me sad that I missed it."

"Oh, you think you feel bad for missing that? You just had a cheater. I had a cheater and a thief. He wiped me out. Took all my cash, took all our savings. Took everything. And then when he was able to get the better lawyer, I could only fight for full custody. Couldn't fight for the house, or even my dining room table. It's fine though, we're making do. We're starting over. And you're helping. So I must stop being grumpy about it and be grateful."

My lips twitched. "Why do I feel that you would rather be anything but grateful right now?"

"Because we like yelling at each other?" Ava asked with a sigh. "I just really need the job. And a place where Faith can grow up. I know that's not going to be here forever. But for the semester, I'll take it."

"Let's make sure that we figure things out, okay? I'm not going to kick you out like he did." I growled at that and Ava's eyes widened. "And I know that you probably would've kicked his ass if you weren't scared to lose custody of Faith."

"If I would've fought harder, he would've taken her. Even though he clearly doesn't want her." She winced, her face going pale. "Which makes me sound like a dumbass. Forever loving him."

"I was his friend too. So, let's not talk about him anymore under this roof. Makes me sick. And I have a long day."

She smiled then. "Sounds like a plan."

"Let's go through the motions." I gestured her behind the bar, and she frowned at the newly painted side.

"What happened here?"

I winced, realizing that I needed to mention this.

"We had a break-in a few nights ago."

Her eyes widened. "What? What happened? Was anyone hurt? Oh my God. Is Faith safe where she is?"

I held up my hands. "Faith is perfectly safe. In fact, because she's in the main inn, she's in the safest place with the amount of security and steps that we've taken over the years. However, since this side is open to the public, apparently somebody was able to rig the door-knob to get in. My brothers and cousins have already fixed that and added additional security measures."

"You were here?" she asked as her eyes widened. "That's why you were walking so stiffly. And the bruises."

I shrugged, then immediately regretted the action. "Yeah. I'm fine though. Just felt like shit for a while. They're not going to get in here to hurt you. I promise."

I hadn't meant for that to sound like a growl, and she swallowed hard. "Okay. I mean, this place already looks safer than the diner."

"I'm never going back there again, by the way. The eggs aren't worth it."

"Well, I don't think I'm welcome back. So we're doing great there."

I sighed, then gestured towards the bar.

"Let's go over the back end, and then we can start on the manager parts. You'll be okay. You've got this."

"Why do I feel like you're reassuring yourself more than me?"

"I have no idea what you're talking about," I teased.

We went through the bar, the taps, our menu, the

computer system. I introduced her to a few of the staff members, who all nodded in greeting, as well as the cook in the back. We went to the distillery side and her eyes widened at the machinery as I introduced her to Sam.

By the time we were done, she kept shaking her head, her notes detailed.

"This place is amazing."

"We're the newest addition. The spa is newly rebuilt after a huge storm we had a couple of years ago. But the winery? That's old school, and brilliantly detailed. You should go take a tour. I'm sure the Wilder women will indoctrinate you soon."

"That doesn't sound scary at all."

"Just a little."

We went to the back storage room, as I showed her where a few of the setups were.

"You'll be doing inventory a lot, but I'll do it with you a few times just so you can get the hang of it."

"I can do this," she said, her voice fierce. "I can."

"I know you can. You kept our trips in tip-top shape, and we were always on time. Which is saying something because Isabelle was always late." I winced. "Sorry."

"We really can't stop saying their names. It's like Beetlejuice."

"Let's not summon them again."

I laughed and went to leave the storage room, only to realize that the door was locked.

"Fuck. I forgot that I needed to replace this."

"What are you talking about?" Ava asked, her voice going a little strained.

"We might be locked in. But don't worry, we'll just bang on the door until someone gets us out."

"Are you kidding me right now?"

Ava slid between me and the door and put her hand on the doorknob. "I have to get to Faith." She tried to twist it, but it wouldn't budge. "What kind of place are you running here?"

"We knocked into the doorknob with a huge crate once, and it put it off-kilter. I need to replace it. Or at least tell my brothers to. I've got it."

But she was pressed against me, her ass right against my cock. It was hard to think because she kept moving and rubbing against me. I could smell her—the honey-sweet scent of her hair.

What the hell was wrong with me?

And then she turned, her ass sliding against my dick again, and then her breasts were against my chest, and she was looking up at me.

When her mouth parted, her eyes going wide, her pupils dilating, I realized that this was a mistake.

I swallowed hard, looking down at her. I had my hands braced on either side of her head, but I hadn't meant to do that. She had shifted between me and the door. This was all her damn fault.

"Oh."

And then she licked her lips.

That little tongue darted out and I swallowed hard, my gaze transfixed.

My pulse raced, and the heat between us intensified.

"You guys okay in there?" Sam called from the other side of the door, and I immediately backed up as Ava ran her hands down her thighs and moved to the side.

"Yeah, you mind letting us out?"

"You need to get that fixed, boss," Sam said as he easily opened the door from the other side.

He looked between us, eyebrows raised.

I shrugged. "Well, got to love locking the new assistant manager in the storage room so she knows how much we actually need the help," I said with a laugh.

Sam joined in. "Sorry about that, Ava. I guess that's first up on fixing?" he asked.

"Yes, it's already on my notes," Ava said as she walked past us. "Thanks for everything today, Wyatt. I need to go see Faith."

"No problem. See you tomorrow."

And then she was gone, and Sam was giving me a look.

"What?" I snapped.

"I didn't say anything. But that sounds like trouble."

"Are you talking about me? Or the new assistant manager."

"I'm not saying anything else."

Then Sam walked off, leaving me alone and wondering what the fuck had just happened.

I had no idea, but it was never going to happen again.

Never.

CHAPTER FIVE
AVA

I had made a few disastrous choices and had near-misses in my life, and yet yesterday felt like one of the worst.

Almost kissing my new boss? A terrible mistake.

Almost kissing my ex-husband's former best friend? Disastrous.

The fact that Wyatt and Isabelle, the woman who ruined my life, had once been married? Catastrophic.

If I had kissed Wyatt, or let him kiss me, it would have ruined everything.

I was such a damn idiot.

I didn't even like him.

Of course I didn't like him. He was Wyatt Wilder. The temperamental nice guy who was giving me a chance, and here I was, trying to ruin it with my stupid hormones.

Maybe it hadn't been a near kiss. Maybe it had just been a bout of claustrophobia because I had been locked in a very small room with him.

Though I felt his cock hardening against my ass when I hadn't even realized I was touching him. Which wasn't something I was ever going to think about again because that was such a stupid mistake.

I could still feel the long length of him against my butt when I swiveled between him and the door.

I am sure it was just my imagination. And even if it wasn't, it was just a normal biological reaction because I had invaded his space.

I was not going to blame myself for this, I was going to blame him. This had to be his fault. Because if I took responsibility for it, then I would have to remember I had licked my damn lips.

Who the hell licked their lips when they were in close company of a man staring at you like that?

And then my breasts had pressed against his body, my nipples hardening.

That was just because it had been way too long since I'd had an orgasm.

When was I supposed to get one? Aaron had been good at giving them to me many years ago, hence why I had continued to sleep with him and why we had Faith.

But then he'd sort of kept missing the spots and pretending to try his best. I hadn't realized that he had been saving his best for Isabelle, but I wasn't going to think about that woman.

That woman who was breaking me.

No, there was no need.

Because she wasn't breaking me.

I was not broken.

My lip quivered but I bit down hard, the pain helping me push down any anxiety.

Because fuck that.

Isabelle hadn't broken me; Aaron hadn't broken me. And Wyatt wasn't going to either.

So, I hadn't had an orgasm in longer than I cared to admit, since before the divorce and everything.

I needed to find that dusty vibrator of mine, wash it off, and see what I could do.

Or maybe just use the shower head because there was a very nice shower head in the cabin.

I looked around the small cabin that was now mine and Faith's home for the time being, and wondered exactly what I was doing.

I was relying on others because I couldn't support my child by myself.

And here I was, being selfish and thinking about orgasms.

No, I didn't need orgasms. I didn't need a man.

I just needed a job and to keep Faith safe.

She was all that mattered in this crazy world of whatever the hell I was doing.

"Mom!"

"Faithy Faith! Did you brush your teeth?" I asked as Faith ran into me, her body slamming hard into mine. When she wrapped her arms around my waist, I laughed and brushed her hair back a bit from her face.

"Yep. See?" She breathed into my face just like she had when she was little, and I smelled the mint of her toothpaste.

"Well, that's good. Are you ready for puzzle time?" I asked.

I had to work that night, so Faith would be with Aurora and the others, and while that was a very scary thing for me, Faith was excited. She had already met the other kids in Wyatt's family, and they immediately clicked. It didn't matter that she was older, she had gone into her teacher mode and all of them played together. I still couldn't believe this was working out so far, so I couldn't mess it up by having any weird tension with Wyatt.

That would ruin everything.

And because I had to work tonight, I was spending the morning with Faith for family time, and then we would go on a walk, and I would do some research to make sure

I could do this job well. If I could, and I thought maybe if I tried hard enough I might, I'd be able to save so I could get us a better place in the same school district, because I liked this school district for Faith, and I wouldn't have to rely solely on the Wilders. I was leaning far too close to resentment for my own good, so I wasn't going to allow that to happen. At least not about the whole family.

Maybe just to Wyatt. Because it was easier doing that than anything else. Not that I was going to think about why that was the case.

No, that would make things a little too difficult for me.

For everyone.

"We're almost done with that one puzzle. But it was easy. For babies."

"Well, we wanted to start off slower in a new home."

"That's okay. Aurora's going to help me with a bigger puzzle at the inn. I love it there. It's so pretty. And everyone's so nice. And all of the guys look like Uncle Wyatt. They're pretty." She fluttered her eyelashes, and I held back a grimace.

My baby girl was starting to look at boys. At eight. Not that she knew what that meant, but she had her little childhood crushes on her favorite kid show, and she was a damn flirt.

I was not ready for her pre-teen years, nor her teen years. But we would grow into them together.

"They do all look similar," I conceded.

We finished our puzzle, ate a snack, and I relished in my daughter's laugh.

Her father hadn't called her in three weeks. And the last call had been short and to the point, and while my baby hadn't cried, she had complained of a stomachache. I'd had the following day off work because of the diner not letting me get overtime, so I took her out of school and we had mommy and daughter time. I didn't know if it was the right way to handle things. Frankly I didn't know if there were any right ways to handle these things.

But I was trying. I didn't have another choice. It felt like I was failing her with every step that I took.

It wasn't fair to my daughter that her father was turning into a terrible human being. And somehow that felt like my fault because I had chosen him.

He hadn't called, he didn't answer texts, but I knew he was around. I saw him on social media with Isabelle.

Just like I had seen Isabelle flash her new diamond ring. One paid for with our money. They were getting married. Isabelle was going to be my baby girl's stepmother and there was nothing I could do.

I wondered if Wyatt knew. He probably did. But he

didn't seem to let it bother him. If anything, he just went about his day, and here I stood, feeling left behind.

"Should we go for a walk?" Faith asked and I smiled.

"Yes, but no petting chickens. They won't like it, baby."

"What about a goat?"

I winced. "Let's talk to East and the others to see. I don't think it's a petting zoo. I think it's just for goat milk."

Not that I knew what they did with the goat milk. Nor did I know why they even had animals. It had to be some form of package deal with the retreat. I didn't know enough about the Wilders and how they worked, but I was going to learn. If I was going to be part of this process and not fail, I had to learn who they were. Which meant I needed to get my head out of my ass, and not think about what happened in the utility room, nor think about Aaron.

Just because my ex-husband didn't call his daughter, didn't make me a failure as a mother.

And if I kept saying those words, it wouldn't feel like a lie.

My phone rang, and for a moment I thought maybe it was Aaron. I didn't want to hear his voice, I didn't want to have any contact with him, but he was still my baby's father. And he was hurting her by ignoring her.

But it wasn't Aaron. Instead, my mother's face filled the screen as I answered.

"Grandma!" Faith called out as she sat on my lap and held the phone with me.

"There are my two girls! I'm sorry I haven't called in a few days. Bradley and I had that hiking trip you know, though it was more glamping, and for all the glamping they said they'd have, the wireless wasn't as great as I wanted. I'm sorry."

I smiled, thinking about how happy my mother looked. She deserved to be happy. After everything she had gone through, everything that she had sacrificed to raise me, even when everything had been taken from her, she deserved it. She deserved this time and peace with her new husband. I liked Bradley, but I hated that he was Canadian and had a beautiful house up there with everything that my mother could ever want. He had taken my mother from me, but I wasn't going to act petulant about it. My mother was happy. And she deserved to be happy. And if I could be one-tenth of the mother to my daughter that my mother was to me, then I would count that as a success.

That was why my mother didn't know most of what had happened with Aaron. She just knew that my marriage had failed and that I had custody of Faith. She didn't know about the money, the crying at night, or the new job.

"We knew you were going camping, that's why we weren't too nervous about you not calling right away," I teased.

"I know, but I like to bug you all the time. I miss my babies. How are you doing, my Faith?"

"I'm doing amazing. I can't wait to see you for Christmas."

I stiffened, having forgotten my mother was planning on visiting for Christmas. I had been nervous as all hell about her coming to my shitty apartment, but how was I going to explain that I lived on the Wilders' compound and didn't pay rent? I didn't have an explanation for that, but thankfully my mother just giggled and clapped her hands much in the same way Faith did.

"Oh, I'm so excited. Bradley and I were thinking about staying at a retreat down there. He has friends who had a reservation at this resort thing and need to cancel, but instead of doing that we thought we would take over the reservation. It's the Wilders, I think?"

I stiffened.

"That's where we are!" Faith said excitedly.

My mother frowned. "What do you mean?" Mom asked, confused.

"I got a new job. A better one," I corrected. "I work for the Wilders now and it comes with housing." Not quite a lie, but it did skirt over a bunch of issues.

My mom blinked. "All of this happened in the last few days?"

"The Wilders get things done," I hedged.

My mom studied my face, and I knew she knew I was leaving things out. I always had. But I wasn't going to budge on this. My mom did not need to worry about me anymore. She did not need to sacrifice for me anymore. I was keeping Faith safe. And if there was anything my mother could do from Canada, she would. But I didn't want her to give up her retirement pension to fix my mistakes.

"Oh. Well, that's great then. I'll have Bradley change over the reservation and we can all stay together for Christmas. I can't wait to see you both. Bradley's out with his daughter right now looking at new cars." She rolled her eyes. "Marie went by herself, and the guy tried to haggle her to the point that she got frustrated and yelled at the man. So now Bradley's going so his daughter has someone to rely on even though she can and wants to do it herself. I just love their relationship."

I smiled and laughed. "So, Marie needs witnesses because she doesn't want to get arrested for beating up some man who thinks that the little lady can't handle it?"

"You know it. She can handle it on her own, and Bradley likes to pretend that he's there to help. Either way, they'll have a good afternoon, and we'll talk about

Christmas when he gets home. Because I want to hear everything. *Everything*, Ava."

I smiled, ignoring the twinge of guilt. "And Marie's okay with you guys not being there for Christmas?"

"We were here for their Thanksgiving, because it's in October, you know," she told Faith.

"I know. I think it's great. That way you can have all the holidays."

"Exactly," Mom said. "So we get Christmas and New Year's with you. It's time. I miss my babies."

"We miss you too, Grandma." Faith went on about how she couldn't wait to see the chickens and the goats, and my mom smiled and nodded, asking all the right questions.

I felt like a failure. But I wasn't going to let myself dwell. I didn't have time. I needed to learn how to do this new job so I could get on my feet again.

I didn't have time to worry about all the stresses.

We ended the phone call and Ava and I went on our walk, sadly not seeing the chickens and goats because we had gone the wrong way on a very big piece of land, then Faith went to play video games and I had a thousand things to do before starting my first shift.

My phone rang again, and I dreaded it. It wasn't going to be Aaron, but maybe it was another debt collector. Because that would be great.

Instead, my childhood friend's name popped up on the screen, and relief poured through me.

"Rory," I said. "I've missed you."

"I've missed you too, babe," my friend said back. "I can't wait to see you. It feels like it's been ages."

I leaned back against my headboard, books and papers and my old nearly broken laptop sprawled all over the bed with me. "I've missed you too. I'm glad that you moved back."

"Same. It's not exactly how I planned on it, but we're making it work. Are you okay, Ava? You just left me a quick message saying that you got a new job and a new address for emergencies, but you didn't explain anything."

For some reason tears threatened, but I swallowed them back. I would not cry. That would make me weak. And I didn't have time or patience to be weak.

"It's a good job. Just a new one. Whenever you get back in town and settled, and you're unpacked at your new apartment, we will talk it over. I promise. Over wine. The Wilders have good wine."

"Yes, we need to talk. Because I've missed you. And I've missed that little girl of yours. She needs to get to know her Aunt Rory."

My heart raced, tears threatening again, but I just smiled and listened to her talk about her new job and new move. I knew Rory was rambling so I didn't have to talk about my own issues. But she would get the truth out of me soon. She was that good.

When we hung up, promising to see each other soon, I let my phone fall to the side, my hands shaking.

Faith was in her room, I could hear her laughing over her tablet, and I would go check on her soon. Just like I would work that night, and I would save money, and I would do all the steps that I needed to be a good mom.

Nothing was like I planned. I put my hands over my face, my shoulders shaking as a breakdown threatened, but I swallowed it back.

I would not cry. I would not break.

I would just live. And fight for my daughter.

I didn't have time to be the broken shell and shattered remains of what I had once been. I would just be this glued and taped-up representation of her. Because that was all I had left.

I didn't have time for tears.

I only had time to move on, and to keep my daughter safe and happy.

There was nothing left for me. And I was okay with that.

CHAPTER SIX

WYATT

"So, how's it going with Ava?"

I pinched the bridge of my nose as I glared at the phone.

How Gabriel, who wasn't even in the state, knew Ava was working for me, I didn't know. Okay, I did know because my brothers were all gossips. Which was weird because we had spent so much of our lives not living on top of each other like we were now. It wasn't that we hadn't spoken to each other often, it was that we had our own lives.

At the time, we'd been in our own heads, trying to keep above water: Gabriel trying to form a band and get into the music industry; Ridge working in places I'd rather not know; me getting a business degree so I could figure out how to own and operate different bars;

and Brooks living his own life and building fantastic architecture.

We had all lived our lives, but now three of us were practically living next door to each other, while Gabriel was in on all the gossip.

"She's doing fine. She's a great bartender. People seem to like her."

It had been a few days since she started working for us, days since that near kiss that I did not want to think about.

We were heading into the Christmas holiday soon, with the different holiday rushes and all the parties that the property held, as well as the family. Ava was taking it in stride, and seeing Faith run around the retreat along-side her mom or one of the Wilder women made me smile. Faith was a hoot and wanted to learn everything.

I wanted to kick Aaron's ass for daring to harm that little girl. Oh, I didn't think there was any physical abuse, but emotional? Fuck Aaron. And fuck everything that he had ever done to harm that child. As well as Ava, but I was better off not thinking about Ava.

"Any sparks?"

There was a crash and a yell on the other side of Gabriel's line, giving me a moment to wonder where the hell that had come from, as Gabriel dealt with what-ever was happening.

"She works for me. There're no sparks."

"That isn't a reason why there could be no sparks. I don't know, you and Ava always had that enemies-to-lovers thing going on."

I sat on my bar stool, the small cabin I had on the property finally feeling like home after a few years. We had retrofitted a few things in the kitchen so it felt a little bit more mine, though I didn't cook often. It was easier just to have dinner at the bar and grill since I was there so often anyway. And it wasn't like I really had women here. I had been married to Isabelle for so long that I had no idea how to date now. And during the time I had been waiting for my divorce to be finalized, it was just too annoying to explain that while I wasn't yet divorced, I'd been separated long enough that Isabelle and Aaron had their own house and lives.

It was weird to think that though we had been separated for over two years and trying to finalize a divorce for a year of that, it was all over. I could have over anyone I wanted. It annoyed me that the first name that came to mind was Ava's.

Damn it. I did not need to think about her. I blamed Gabriel for this.

"Wait, enemies to lovers?" I asked, finally clicking in on what Gabriel had said.

My brother snorted. "Yes. You guys fought all the

time. At least that's what I saw the few times I met her."

I scowled, remembering those times. It had been when Isabelle invited people over for a barbecue or group dinner, and I had been manning the grill, annoyed when Ava had come over to tell me exactly what I was doing wrong. The fact that I had overcooked the chicken on one side of the grill because I'd had the flames too high was not my fault. It was her fault for distracting me.

Gabriel had shown up to a few of those, and everybody had swooned over the little brother that was a Grammy winner and had sold-out concerts. It was hard to believe that Gabriel, with the voice of an angel but sin of a rock star, was so famous but was still my punky little brother who loved needling me.

Case in point, about Ava.

"We're not enemies, I guess we're learning to be friends. But we're sure as fuck not lovers."

"I'm thinking you're protesting a little too much."

"What is that noise?" I asked after I heard what sounded like broken glass and a guitar riff behind Gabriel. It was still decently early for me, almost afternoon, but considering I worked until around two a.m., this *was* my morning.

Of course, I didn't keep Gabriel's rock star hours, so what did I know. Some part of me knew I should be worried about him, but Gabriel made good decisions and he asked for help when he needed it. So I would just keep an eye on him. Just like the rest of my family was doing.

"One of my bandmates knocked over a vase with flowers in it, and now another one is trying to distract our manager by playing music while they clean it up. It's fun."

I paused, wondering if what he said was true. "Everything okay there?" I asked, my voice soft.

Gabriel was silent for so long I was afraid either nothing was okay, or he was annoyed that I had even asked.

"Yes. Everything's good. Just a long night prepping for this next segment of the tour. I'm not even hungover or anything. It's what happens when I don't drink during huge tour setups."

"As an owner of a distillery, I'm proud of you," I teased, relief pouring in. Gabriel didn't lie to me, and I was grateful for that.

"It's just going to be a long few months. You guys are coming out though, right?"

"You know it. Although I don't know if we can make it all out at the same time with our work schedules. But we have plans."

"Just call my manager if you need tickets and you can't get a hold of me. You know, because I'm out living the rock star life. Tons of women and drugs, according to the tabloids."

"Yes, I'm sure that's the case," I said dryly. "What's the latest rumor?"

"That Lark and Bethany and I are having a massive poly three-way and both of their husbands, you know our cousins, are watching."

Lark and Bethany were each married to one of our Wilder cousins, and they had known each other as well as Gabriel outside of our family before Lark and Bethany had married in. I always thought that was pretty cool because we had a couple of Grammy winners and an Oscar winner in our midst. I didn't get too starstruck often, mostly because I knew what happened behind the scenes with Gabriel, but Lark and Bethany? I did have to blink a bit when I first met them.

"I'll be sure to tell the cousins hi from you and sorry for their loss."

"Oh, don't worry, I text them often just to make sure they know."

I laughed at that, shaking my head. "You're a menace."

"I really am. Hey, I've got to go. But tell the little squirt hi for me."

"Are you talking about Ava or Faith?" I teased.

"Don't let Ava hear you saying that or she's going to kick your ass. And I believe she can."

"We both know she'd win in a fight," I said. "Be safe, check in."

"As always, Mom," Gabriel said, before signing off.

I put my phone in my joggers, before rolling my shoulders back, then cleaned out my coffee mug before putting in my headphones and starting to stretch. I wanted to go out for a jog before the weather changed since there was another cold front coming through, and then I had to head into work and see how Ava did that morning on inventory.

She was already doing loads better than my former assistant manager, and none of the staff seemed to resent the fact that I'd brought in outside help. Though none of the staff had wanted her job to begin with.

I locked up behind me and started to jog down the path, my muscles aching from the long night of work before. I was in shape, and I worked out, but I probably did the least compared to my brothers. Considering one was a security specialist, one worked with his hands for a living, and one sweated buckets onstage nearly every night, yeah, I had to work out a little bit harder since my job sometimes sat me on my ass for hours a day.

I kept running to the other side of the property, through the path of cedar and mesquite trees. Out here there were no other people. Unless they were on the path as well, it was deserted. Especially at this time of day and this time of year. It had rained a couple nights before, so it was still muddy in patches, but it was pleasant. You could hear whatever birds were left in Texas this time of year in the trees and the water pouring through the creek a little ways away.

The Wilder Retreat had over a hundred acres of land, and most of it would never be used other than for things like this. We weren't going to add a golf course that sucked up water during droughts, and we weren't going to add tons of developments that stained the landscape. This was what my cousins wanted when they first bought the place after they got out of the military, and I was just grateful I was now part of it. Something bigger than myself.

I kept moving, my feet confidently going over the trail. It was a bit rocky, but it wasn't too bad. East and Brooks made sure the trail was taken care of, but still looked rustic enough that it wasn't an eyesore.

I wanted to make it to a scenic view area and sit around for a bit, just relax before I had to get through my day.

When I turned the corner, I was surprised to see I wasn't the first person to think of this spot.

Ava sat on a wooden bench, knees tucked up under her chin, and my heart raced.

What the hell was that about?

My heart did not race when it came to her.

Her gaze shot to mine as I tried to be as loud as possible, taking out my earphones so I could hear her.

Eyes wide, she put her hand over her chest.

"What the fuck. You scared me."

"Well, you startled me too. I didn't realize you'd be out here."

"What, you own this bench?" she asked.

I could see something had upset her, maybe it was me, but I didn't care. I hated that I could hear Gabriel's voice in my head, saying the word "lovers" when it came to her.

I had done my best never to think about Ava that way. Our entire acquaintance I had never done that, and yet here I was, thinking about her naked.

I wanted to know what color her nipples were.

Who the hell thought those things?

"I'm just out here for a jog. Didn't realize you'd be out here either. I was here first."

"Excuse me, I was sitting here first. Just go away, Wyatt."

"I don't think I will. What's wrong, Ava?"

She scowled at me. "Nothing's wrong."

"Where's Faith?"

"Rory picked her up for a fun afternoon."

I frowned. "Rory?" Why did I get jealous? Was Rory some dude? Did Ava have a boyfriend?

"My friend from school? I think you met her. I don't remember. But they're out."

"Oh."

Why did I feel relieved at that?

"I was just sitting here, trying to relax, and then I heard you stomping your way down the path. Panting."

"Are you calling me out of shape?" I asked. I didn't know why I did it, but I lifted my sweatshirt up so she could see my rock-hard abs. "See? Not out of shape."

Her gaze went to my bare skin, and she did that thing again. She licked her fucking lips.

"What the hell is wrong with us?" I asked, my voice low. "Like what you see?" I teased, needling her.

"You're an asshole." She let her feet drop from the bench before she turned away from me, moving back down the path.

Annoyed, I followed her. "What? You're the one who was licking your lips at the sight of me."

"You're so full of yourself," she grumbled, not stopping.

I followed her, my pace easily able to keep up with her walk. "What is wrong with you today? Sleep on the wrong side of the bed?"

"Like I have time to sleep." She rolled her eyes, and I gripped her arm gently and turned her to face me.

"Ava. Talk to me."

"Wyatt, I really don't want to talk."

When her gaze went to my mouth, I wondered what she would do. What she wanted to do.

So I did the one thing I shouldn't and lowered my mouth to hers.

She didn't back away, didn't stop me. Her hand gripped my sweatshirt and tightened. Her lips parted underneath mine as I licked her tongue. I slid my hand from her arm to her hair, tugging so I could tilt her head and deepen the kiss. I slid my other hand down her hips and squeezed her ass. She was more than a handful, soft and full. I couldn't help but groan again as she continued to kiss me back. I didn't know what happened, but then we were both moving towards a tree, her back against it.

"This is a mistake," she whispered against my lips.

"A huge fucking mistake," I whispered back. But we didn't stop. I tugged at her leggings, pulling them down past her knees. Her hands were underneath my shirt, then pulling at my joggers, shoving them down.

I was already hard, moisture at the tip.

"This is so wrong," she repeated.

"Tell me to stop."

She met my gaze and I saw the anger there, but I didn't think it was directed at me.

But there was that heat, that tension, and I didn't want to stop.

So she kicked one foot, her leggings pulling free, and

I did what I needed to. I kissed her again. She slid her hand between us, gripping the base of my cock. I groaned, my eyes shut, but it was hard to breathe. When she began to stroke me, squeezing down at the base and then sliding up and down the shaft, I licked my lips, then hers. I slid my hand between us, moving her panties to the side. She was wet and hot. I slid my middle finger between her folds, parting them softly.

"You want me."

"Don't get a big head about it."

"You're already holding my big head," I teased.

She squeezed my shaft.

"Temptress."

"Just finger me already," she ordered.

"As my lady commands," I murmured, before fucking her mouth with my tongue, and spearing her with two fingers. She groaned, arching her body as my palm pressed against her mound and my middle and ring fingers fucked her. I moved in and out of her, the sound of her wetness echoing along the forest. We had to be quick, careful. Anybody could come up on us at any moment.

And I didn't care.

The icy wind chilled my ass and I ignored it but I didn't want her to get cold, so I'd have to find a way to keep her warm.

I continued to fuck her with my hand, loving the

way she rode me, and when she tightened around me, her mouth parting, I took her scream into my mouth so it wouldn't echo in the canyon. And she came, her whole body shivering.

And then her free leg was wrapped around my hip, bringing me closer.

She pulled at my cock, pressing it against her entrance. I took her mouth, and then I took her.

I slammed into her in one thrust, her wet cunt squeezing around my cock.

"Who's fucking you right now," I growled against her lips. "Tell me who's fucking you."

"I can fuck myself," Ava teased, rolling her hips along my dick.

I knew her back had to be hurting against the tree, but I didn't care. I needed her to say my name.

"Who's fucking you right now?" I asked, my voice pointed.

"You are. At least you were. Get moving."

I grinned, taking her mouth.

I picked up her other leg and wrapped them both around my waist. And then she was holding onto me, and I was doing everything that I could to keep her steady, to keep her back safe from the bark. I kept pounding into her, both of us breathing heavily, until her sweet pussy was coming around my cock again, squeezing me. I couldn't hold back, my orgasm hit me hard, and I finally slid out of her, coming into my hand and over the fallen leaves at our feet.

Both of us shook. I swallowed hard, the ramifications of what we had just done hitting home.

We hadn't used a condom. And I had just fucked my friend in a forest where anyone could have come up to us.

She looked between us, her eyes wide. Wordlessly we shifted so we could pull our clothes back on.

She almost tripped, trying to pull her leggings over her boot, but I reached out to steady her. When she didn't bark at me for helping her, I knew something was wrong.

"Ava?"

She looked at me before bursting into tears, and I caught her as she fell.

Holy fuck.

I had just broken Ava London.

I was a cruel, terrible man.

But seeing her tears? That broke me more than anything. So I settled onto the ground a little ways away from where we had just fucked against a tree and held her while she cried.

I wasn't sure what else I could do. What else I should do.

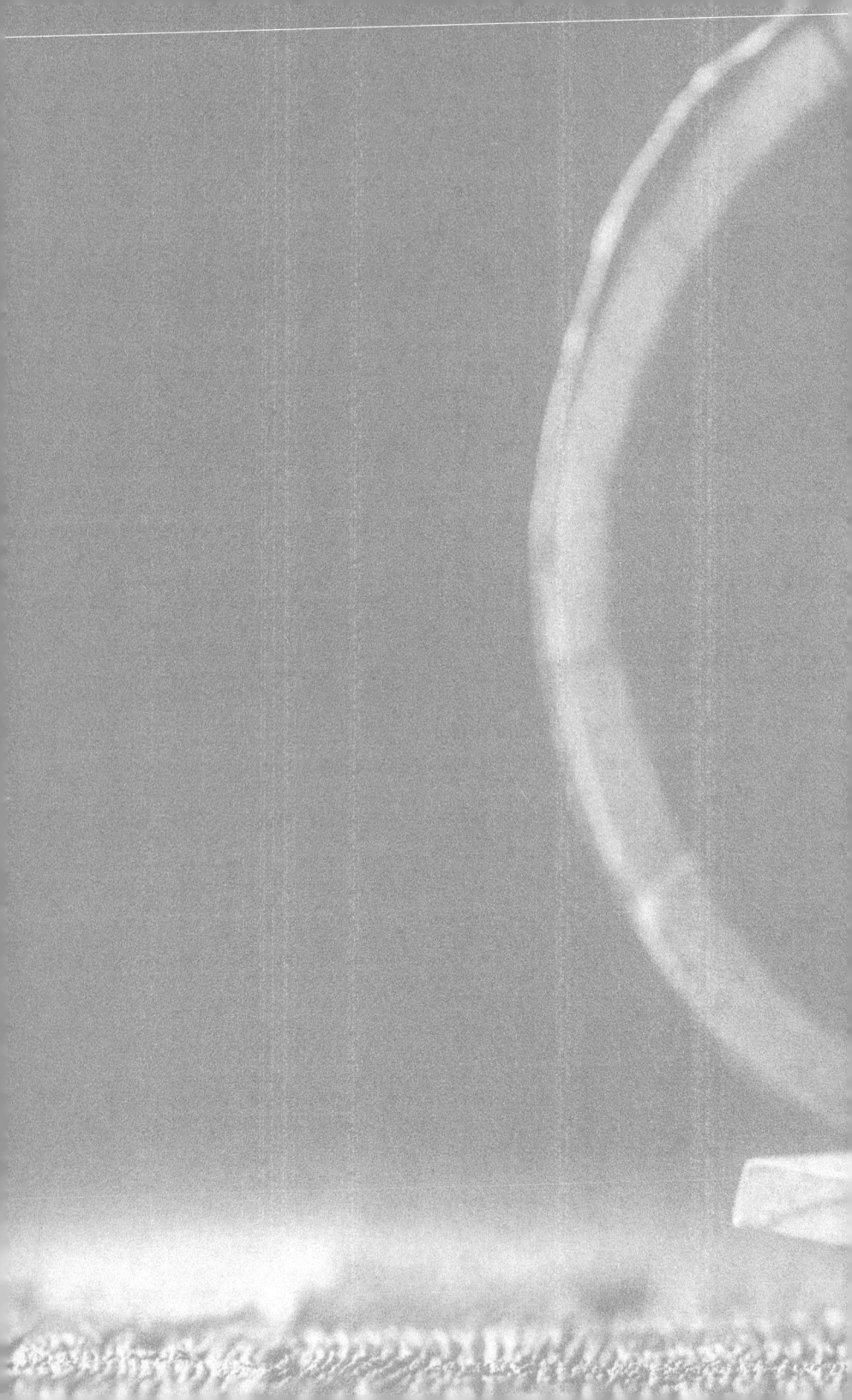

CHAPTER SEVEN
AVA

I needed to stop crying.

I tried to hold everything in but there was nothing I could do.

I could not stop crying.

It was as if everything I had been holding inside for years broke free. An unbearable weight fell onto my shoulders, pushing me down into the abyss. As if dark spindly fingers reached around my throat to grip and never let go.

My shoulders shook, my entire body caving in on itself.

There was no time for breaking down or for making more mistakes, and yet that seemed to be all I was doing.

Faith needed me to be strong. She didn't need a

mom who cried at the drop of a hat and pushed away her daughter's pain to focus on her own. I would not be that person. I needed to be stronger than this. And yet I couldn't stop the sob escaping from my mouth as I tried to suck in a breath.

Wyatt held me tightly, running his hands through my hair as he tried to calm me down.

He hired me to be his assistant manager and bartender, hired me because he felt sorry for me, and now here I was, postcoital bliss, sitting in his lap on the ground while he held me and whispered words I couldn't even hear over my own mental breakdown.

I hated myself with each in-drawn jagged breath, and each exhale that seemed to take the monsters away only to suck them right back in with my every inhale.

I hadn't cried after the divorce, hadn't cried after losing everything. I hadn't had time.

But apparently making one of the worst decisions of my life by having sex with Wyatt in the middle of a damn walking trail had finally broken through. It was one more thing, one more thing I could not handle.

And throughout it all, Wyatt just held me.

I hated myself so much for it.

Finally, snot running out my nose, my cheeks most likely red and splotchy, I was able to take a deep breath and let out a shuddering sigh.

"There you go. There you go."

He sounded as if he were trying to calm an unsteady mare, and maybe that was it. Maybe I was a horse that couldn't handle being led and was ready to buck any minute.

The absurdity and the full reality of the situation began to settle over me and I realized I was sitting on Wyatt's lap, and some part of me didn't want to get up, while the rest of me knew I needed to.

"I'm sorry. I need to, I need to get up."

But Wyatt didn't let me go, instead he tightened his hold.

"Just a minute. You freaked me the fuck out. So let me hold you for my own well-being."

That sounded like a huge lie, so much bullshit, but I let him hold me. For his sake. Even though I knew it wasn't true.

"I don't want to say thank you," I whispered.

He sighed, running his hands down my hair. I didn't like that it felt good.

"That's fine. You don't have to like this. But it sounds to me like you really needed to get it out."

"I really shouldn't have done this."

"You mean having sex out in the woods with me, or crying in my arms?"

I scrambled off him, kneeling in the wet dirt and knowing I looked a wreck.

"Maybe both?"

"Sit down, no one's going to be by for a while. We're in the middle of two large reservations, and my brothers are all working. If Faith is with your friend, then it's just us. Breathe. Talk to me."

Knowing he was going to be relentless about this, and the fact that we probably should talk about the fact that we hadn't used a damn condom, I sighed and sank down into the mud.

"I'm sorry for crying."

"Don't be. I cry too."

I gave him a look. "You break down in people's arms like that?"

"I could. I know my brothers would give me shit but they wouldn't be mad about it. So, where do you want to start?" Wyatt asked. He had his legs folded up, his arms resting on his knees.

I looked at his strong jaw, the stubble covering his cheeks and neck. That stubble hadn't felt bad at all when he had been kissing me, and I wondered if I had beard burn.

"Your face isn't red from my beard," he whispered. That's when I realized I had touched my face while looking at him, and I quickly let my hand fall.

"That can't happen again, Wyatt."

"The crying?" He teased and I flipped him off, grateful for the humor.

"Okay. So we don't have sex in the woods again.

That's fine." He cleared his throat. "I wasn't expecting that, you know. I don't, well, I don't even know why that happened."

I shook my head. "I got tested after Aaron...well. After I found out he was cheating on me. I didn't know if it was just with Isabelle or others. But I'm clean. I can show you the test. They're probably out of date at this point, but I can do another." I swallowed hard.

"I'm clean too. Took the same test because of Isabelle." He cleared his throat. "And I haven't been with anyone since her." He winced. "I don't know if that's supposed to make me sound good or bad. But I hadn't had time to be with a woman in those months, damn, years now." He sighed. "But I'm clean too. I can show you all of that. Or we can just trust each other."

"The last time I trusted someone, he broke my and my baby's hearts," I blurted. Wyatt winced, and that was the crux of the situation.

"I trusted him too, you know."

I looked up at him and realized that we had never talked about this. Everything had happened suddenly, and then the divorces had taken over a year, two years in his case, and there was nothing left. There hadn't been anything left of me to talk to him about.

"I'm on birth control, and Faith was a hard pregnancy."

Wyatt's gaze went to me, his eyes sharpening. "But you're okay?"

I ignored the warmth simmering in my chest. Because Aaron had been so worried about me at first but never worried after. It never occurred to him that I had maybe wanted more children. Or maybe it had, and we just hadn't spoken about it. Maybe my resentment of who he was now meant that I couldn't focus on anything but who he had been then.

I swallowed hard.

"I'm okay. But I have uterine scarring." I winced. "I don't know if you want to hear all that."

"I was just inside you while I pounded you into a tree. I think I can handle it."

I scowled at him, but he was taking this seriously; I saw it in his gaze. Even if he was trying to lighten the mood.

"I'm on birth control, because my IUD never leaves me, and near the end of our marriage I wasn't even sure I wanted to have more children with Aaron."

I didn't even realize I had been thinking those words, but there they were, out there. I hadn't even let myself think those thoughts before.

"I didn't voice that to him, you know. It was just something that happened. And then I couldn't take it back and I can't take those words back."

"You don't need to."

"All of that to say, I'll keep very centered and let you know if anything changes, but it's not the right time for me to get pregnant, and between birth control, and what my doctor says, it's not going to happen."

"I feel like I should say I'm sorry, but then again..." His voice trailed off and I sighed.

"Then again," I repeated.

"I'll get you the test results though."

I nodded. "That can't happen again. I don't even know why it did."

"Because we've been attracted to each other since the beginning, Ava," he said, his voice nearly a growl.

I winced. "Don't say that."

"It's true. You felt it, it's probably why we fought so much."

I scowled at him. "We fought so much because you always thought you were right."

He snorted. "Because I was right most of the time."

"Most, not all. And usually we agreed with each other. It was just easier to fight with you than to fight with Aaron." I winced. "I keep saying things I hadn't even realized were true."

"Aaron was always a competitive asshole. I thought it made him endearing. You know, in that bro sort of way."

"Same, but in the whole 'I married him' sort of way." I let out a breath. "I'm not doing this again. With you or with anyone. I'm going to raise Faith, make sure she has a roof over her head that's something that I can afford. I'm going to put her through school and make sure she's happy and has all the kid experiences. Like her first job or her first car. I'm going to make sure she gets all of that. Because Aaron sure is not going to help, so I must. And I want to. So I can't have my brain going in a thousand different directions like this conversation's going."

"You can do all that and have a life, you know."

My gaze shot to him. "So you're saying you want to sleep together again?" I blurted.

He swallowed hard and didn't answer.

Well. There was that.

I didn't know why I felt the sting of disappointment and rejection. I didn't want to sleep with him either.

"So we don't do this again. We don't talk about it. We just move on. And make it work."

"Fine. We can do that. Do you want to talk about the crying now?"

I shook my head. "No."

"Have you talked to Rory about it?"

"She has her own life to deal with. I'm fine."

"You're clearly not fine, Ava. And why not talk to me about it? I'm literally the only other person that might have an inkling of what you're going through."

I hated that he was right. I hated it all.

I hated that I had trusted the wrong person. That I was attracted to Wyatt. Hated that it felt like I was making the same mistakes. Sleeping with someone who could ruin my life. Who could take everything.

He was my boss, someone who could fire me and rip out my safety net that I was just now rebuilding. He had found me a place to live, but he was also connected to my ex. So when everything went south, I would end up in the same place I'd already been. Sleeping with him had been a mistake, and continuing to would be insanity. So I wouldn't. I wouldn't put myself and Faith in that situation again.

But he was also right.

Because he was probably the only other person in the world besides Faith who knew anything about this. And I was trying to shield Faith from as much of it as possible.

"I hate him so much," I breathed.

Wyatt shifted, and I froze but he didn't touch me. He just sat hip-to-hip with me, a bare inch between us, and his shoulders sagged.

"I hate him too. He was my friend. I trusted him, told him my secrets. And when my brothers were off having lives of their own and we didn't get to see each other every week like I wanted, I had Aaron."

"I'm sorry you lost your best friend."

He looked at me, eyebrow raised. "I'm sorry you lost yours."

I shook my head. "I don't think Isabelle was my best friend," I said.

He frowned. "What do you mean?"

"Isabelle and I hung out when we did the whole ladies who lunch thing, and we hung out when we were at your house or you were at mine, because you and Aaron were friends. But I didn't call Isabelle when I needed to talk about my life or Aaron. I didn't break down in front of her. That was always Rory."

"I didn't know."

"I didn't realize that until I was on the outside looking in and I realized I had no one to talk about Aaron to. I had Rory, but she didn't live close by. Now she does and I can tell her things and it's wonderful, and yet it still breaks me because I didn't have it for all that time. I had no one. And I didn't even realize it because I had buried myself in my own situation. I got pregnant with Faith so I married the man I thought I loved. A man who not only cheated on me, but broke your trust and left my baby girl. He took my money, my security, even my boxes of memories from my childhood. He took everything."

"He took your boxes?" he asked.

"Yes, like my middle school yearbook and photo albums. Everything that had been in the attic, he took it all. I don't even think he realized he did. He was just so intent on ripping everything away to hurt me and Faith that he didn't even care that it wasn't his to begin with."

"I need to go find your lawyer and strangle him since I can't strangle Aaron."

"I don't think you're supposed to strangle anyone."

"True, but I'm still pissed off for you."

That familiar burning rage slid through me, but it was nice to talk about this with someone. "I made mistakes. I trusted Aaron."

"Like I said, so did I. But he doesn't fucking matter anymore."

"He's still Faith's father."

"Being a sperm donor and then walking out doesn't qualify as a father in my book."

My lips twitched even as my heart ached. "True. But Faith asks about him sometimes, and he called once out of the blue. And he's always just on time with his meager child support. So he's still in my life."

"Well, fuck him. If Faith needs to know her dad, you're going to protect her. Hell, we Wilders are going to too. We don't let little kids get hurt because asshole adults don't know how to be a fucking human."

Tears threatened again at the sincerity in his tone, but I didn't let them fall. I had cried enough, thank you very much.

"My goal is to never talk to Isabelle and Aaron again," Wyatt said after a moment. "But if you need to meet with Aaron because he wants to see his kid, or you have paperwork? Let me know, okay?"

I shook my head. "I can handle it on my own."

"You can, but you don't have to. Or call one of my cousins-in-law. Or even one of my brothers or cousins. Hell, any one of us. I know you're worried, because Aaron turned out to be such an asshole, but you've got us now."

"It's really hard to trust that," I said quietly, my worst fears sliding out.

"I know. And that means we'll take this one step at a time."

"And we can never do this again." I waved towards the tree. "Because if I find myself being that stupid again, I won't even be able to trust myself."

"Okay. Then let's just be friends. No more yelling at each other."

"What's the fun in that?" I teased, feeling humor for the first time in a long time.

Wyatt threw his head back and laughed. "Fine. We'll fight. But just because it's fun. But if you need someone to talk to again, to cry with because you can't do it in front of Faith, just let me know." He let out a breath. "For Faith."

"For Faith." I repeated the familiar phrase that I knew meant a lot more than that.

Wyatt stood up and held out his hand.

Part of me wanted to push his hand away and stand up on my own, but I knew that would be just to spite myself. So I slid my hand into his and let him pull me to my feet.

We were both a mess, and looked like we had wrestled on the ground, but I didn't care. Not when everything else was far more important.

"I'll see you at work?" he asked.

I nodded. "You're right. I should go over the inventory."

Back to normal topics. Not about sex or the fact that he had given me one of the best orgasms of my life.

No, none of that.

I dropped my hand quickly and then, with a chin lift and a small smile that I couldn't read, he made his way down the path to finish his run. And because I needed to breathe, I went the opposite direction, back towards the cabin.

Everything that had just occurred had been a terrible mistake. The words, the sex, the breathing, the crying, all of it.

And yet, there was no going back from that.

I hated that somehow, I felt more relieved than anything.

CARRIE ANN RYAN

Because for some reason I wanted to trust him.

I wanted to trust that he heard me, that he understood. That this wasn't the end of my world once again.

And the fact that I wanted to trust him? That told me how big of a mistake it was.

Because trust had gotten me the worst pain of my life and hurt my child.

Trust had broken everything.

So I would never trust again.

Not even Wyatt Wilder and those kind eyes of his.

CHAPTER EIGHT

WYATT

It turns out having sex with your former best friend's ex-wife and your current employee was not great for keeping your mind on tasks.

Who knew?

The fact that it had been one of the best orgasms of my life was not the issue.

Okay, it was so totally the issue, but I wasn't going to think about it anymore.

Because thinking about Ava's wet cunt surrounding my dick while I slid deep inside her meant I had a hard-on while going through the inventory that Ava had just worked through.

Ava. My employee. The woman who broke down into torrential sobs in my arms after we'd had sex.

I could only blame myself.

Okay, I could blame Aaron for it too because he was such a limp-dicked piece of shit. But I had been the one who literally fucked that breakdown out of her.

Not only had we had unprotected sex out in the elements, but we had also bared other things to each other as well.

I wasn't in the mood for fucking metaphors.

I was such a damn idiot and I deserved anything that came my way.

But what I really needed to do was finish my work so I could go see my brothers and not tell them that I had sex with Ava. They would call me all kinds of a fool, and I already knew I was a fool.

I did my best to push Ava and everything out of my mind, because I had shit to do today. I was closing the bar, but I had an early dinner with my brothers. It was nice to have things like that, especially after so many years when we weren't together.

Ridge and Aurora had a trip coming up after Christmas, and then there would be wedding planning and everything that came with that. Of course, the fact that we lived at a wedding venue, and my cousin's wife was a wedding planner, meant we had shit handled. Hopefully I would just have to show up in a tux and say a few words if they wanted me to. Maybe not trip over my own feet. That had only happened once at an event, and I would never live it down.

I pushed all thoughts of the day before out of my mind and went back to work.

I was an hour in, Sam coming in and out, going through paperwork with me, when my phone buzzed.

Thinking it was one of my brothers telling me to get my ass over there, I looked down at the screen and froze.

ISABELLE:

Do you remember that time in Charleston when we went to the restaurant and shared tapas? And you had that cream all over your lip?

ISABELLE:

And then we drank way too much bubbly and mixed it with whiskey and then we took that long walk.

ISABELLE:

Do you remember that?

ISABELLE:

That memory just popped up on my phone, and I wanted to send you those photos.

The next message was a photo of us with her lips on my cheek and such happiness in my eyes that I didn't even recognize myself.

What the fuck was this woman doing?

This was my ex-wife. Texting me memories from a vacation that I didn't want to remember.

Oh, I remembered the meal, and the walk, and the decently okay sex afterwards.

But then I remembered her yelling at me because we didn't get the upgrade to the suite that she wanted. Or that I hadn't worn brown shoes and a belt, rather than black shoes, nice jeans, and no belt. Apparently I was not high-class enough for the restaurant she'd wanted to go to. Not that we even had reservations for it. We'd gone to another place that was damn good and had great reviews, but it hadn't been her perfect place.

Of course, she could have made the reservations if that's what she wanted, or she could have told me what she wanted.

Despite the fact that I tried, I had never been able to read that woman's mind.

But still it did not explain why she was messaging me right now.

I didn't answer her because there was no reason. If I did then I was going to be initiating contact once again, and then I'd have to deal with her responding back, or God forbid Aaron looking at it.

That would be a pain in the ass because if Aaron figured out that Isabelle was texting me, he was going to get the wrong idea.

I wasn't about to play her game.

I hid the text message, and thankfully I didn't have my phone set to where it showed as read or not. She would never know if I saw it, and therefore I could push her out of my mind.

But what the hell.

My phone buzzed again, and as this odd sense of foreboding slid over me, I looked down at the readout before relief slid through me.

BROOKS:

Come on over to the winery. I know it's a longer way for you, but we have cheese. And wine.

My lips twitched as I texted an affirmative and grabbed my things.

"Hey, Sam, I'm heading out."

"No problem. I'll probably be gone by the time you get back, but Ava should be here."

I swallowed hard, my dick getting stiff at just the mention of her.

"No problem. Are you good handling the bar for a little bit?"

"We only have ten minutes until she gets here. Do you want to wait for her?"

Not in the slightest.

"Brooks wants me there now. I'm going to hop in a golf cart and zoom away."

"Just don't get a ticket."

I laughed. "Are they really giving out Wilder tickets on our land?" I asked, heading towards the door.

"Your brother and Trace are having way too much fun zipping around on the security carts. If they could give tickets, they would. At this point they just take the golf carts away from the guests if they are driving recklessly."

"I can't believe they're letting guests have golf carts," I said with a laugh.

"Only a few, though I think it's better for them to have the staff drive them about. Way less liability."

"Amen on that," I said with a laugh.

I headed out to my cart and made my way towards the winery on the other side of the property.

The vines had come with the land from an old chief master sergeant that once owned the place. He had done well with it before my cousins bought the place. And then we had added more of our flair to it. Now we were sprawling over hundreds of acres, but most of it was barren land, which worked for us.

It didn't take long to get to the winery, though it felt like it in the biting wind. I probably should have driven my truck, but I hadn't wanted to deal with the winding roads and finding parking. There were a few events going on, and I just wanted to be able to get in and get out easily.

My phone buzzed again as I parked, and it was another text from Isabelle. I didn't bother reading it.

I didn't know what was going on with her, but I wanted nothing to do with it.

Maybe Isabelle and Aaron were perfect for each other.

I just hated the fact that it had hurt Ava.

And that Isabelle was going to be Faith's stepmother, and Aaron didn't even bother to speak with his own daughter.

I was going to kick that man's ass.

"You're here," Ridge said as he came out of the winery, Brooks by his side. "Come on, we're going for a walk."

I shivered and frowned at them. "I just rode the golf cart over here. I'm freezing."

"I have coffee," Brooks said as he handed me an insulated thermos.

"I still fucking hate you," I replied, even as I grabbed the cup and took a sip. It was hot; I was going to need it. "Why are we going on a walk again?"

"Because I'm about to eat a shitload of pasta and cheese," Ridge said as he slapped his washboard abs. "I need to look good for my woman for the wedding."

I rolled my eyes. "Well, that's great. Good to know that you're thinking about your figure."

"My woman would love whatever I wore or whatever I looked like, but I want to look nice for her."

"You don't need washboard abs for that, you just need to wash your hair," I teased.

"That is true. Anyway, how's your day going?"

I nearly blurted that not only had I fucked Ava, but my ex had texted me, but neither one of those sounded like a good thing to share. Instead I talked about work, and a new label we were working on for the upcoming release of our next batch. Ridge had questions, and Brooks just stood by, silent and listening. Brooks was getting more and more silent these days and it worried me, but he had his reasons. We all knew why.

We kept walking up the path when a familiar laugh hit my ears and I smiled despite myself.

"Uncle Wyatt!" Faith called as she ran towards me, full tilt. I handed Brooks my coffee cup and held out my arms.

"Faith!"

She jumped into my arms, and I staggered back, mostly because she had trusted me so much she hadn't stopped moving and her momentum was a bit much.

I twirled her around as she laughed and kicked, and I kissed her on the top of her head as I set her down.

"What are you doing out here?" I asked, only just now realizing that she was out on the property alone.

Ava was at work, so where the hell was the person watching her?

"Faith!" an unfamiliar voice called, and I held on to Faith's hand.

"Faith!" the voice asked again, this time a bit more panicked.

A woman with long blond hair flowing behind her came around the corner, running full speed, panic in her gaze.

The sight of Faith holding my hand and standing beside two other big hulking men probably scared the shit out of her.

"Faith! You know not to run off like that."

"Sorry, Aunt Rory," Faith said as she squeezed my hand. "Uncle Wyatt, this is Aunt Rory." She looked over at Rory, and a vague recollection of a photo I had once seen of the other woman hit. That's who that was. Ava's childhood friend, who was here to stay and was apparently spending some time with Faith.

I wondered if Rory knew what had happened between me and Ava. Not that it would be wrong if she did. Ava was allowed to tell whoever she wanted, but we had wanted to keep this to ourselves, right? Hell, we hadn't made a pact about that. We had just said it wouldn't happen again and we wouldn't talk about it. We hadn't said we wouldn't tell anyone else.

Holy fuck. Was Rory about to kick me in the balls? I

wouldn't blame her. I had just fucked her best friend and probably shouldn't have.

Rory's shoulders relaxed though, and she didn't look like she wanted to kill me. So that had to count as a win.

"Oh, Wyatt. I recognize you from a photo now."

The photo had to have been with Aaron though, so I saw the anger in her eyes.

But then she did the weirdest thing. She looked over at Brooks, her eyes widening.

"Brooks?" she asked, her voice a whisper.

Brooks stiffened, and I hadn't realized that he hadn't said a damn word. Ridge looked between us, as if watching the tableau and confused as hell right along with me.

"Rory? I didn't know you were Ava's Rory. Or I guess Faith's Rory."

Rory cleared her throat. "It's been a while."

"Yeah, it has."

They didn't say anything else.

What the hell?

Brooks had been married once and lost his wife, which was something that we as a family didn't mention because it hurt Brooks to talk about. But when on earth had he met Rory? Before? After?

How was this all connected, and how was this the biggest thing that had happened, and not me and Ava?

Not that there was a me and Ava.

I quickly pushed everything from my mind and took a deep breath.

"I see you guys are out for a walk," I said into the silence, feeling awkward as hell.

"Yes. I love walking. And now Aunt Rory and I are going to go shopping. Because I want to buy something for Christmas for Mommy. She deserves it."

I smiled then, squeezing her hand.

"You're right. She does."

"Anyway, sorry to interrupt your walk," Rory said, holding out her hand. "Come on, Faith. We're going to have another talk about you running off and talking to strangers."

"They're not strangers," Faith replied, walking away with Rory.

"Just strange," Ridge and I said at the same time before looking at each other and bursting out laughing.

Brooks was silent.

What the fuck.

"Anyway. Nice to see you, Brooks. And I guess you're Ridge?" she asked. "I know who Gabriel is."

Ridge laughed. "Everyone knows who Gabriel is."

"Anyway, we've got to go. Have fun on your walk."

"Bye, Wyatt, bye, Ridge, bye, Brooks, bye, everyone!" Faith called out, and then started talking a thousand miles a minute about the book she had been reading with Rory.

The fact that that little girl could switch between ten different conversations at once had me standing there in awe.

"So, Faith is a hoot," Ridge put in, and I sighed before taking my coffee back from Brooks, who still hadn't said a damn thing.

"Yeah, she's great, isn't she?" I added.

"So, you want to talk about it?" Ridge asked, and I was grateful that he broached the subject.

Brooks seemed to shake himself out of his stupor and let out a breath. "Sorry, it's been a while since I saw Rory. Not since, I don't know, a few months after the funeral. It wasn't anything like you're thinking," he added. "It was just a flash from the past I wasn't expecting. Weird that she's friends with Ava though."

"Childhood friends that kept in touch," I corrected. "So it makes sense that she would have different friend groups."

Brooks gave me a weird look. "Yeah, you're right. I just wasn't expecting to ever see her again. Memories and shit, you know?"

I sipped my coffee and nodded. "Oh yeah, you don't have to tell me twice."

"You okay?" Ridge asked, and Brooks nodded.

"Yeah. And I don't know why I acted like that either.

It's just weird when things from your past slap you in the face when you aren't expecting them."

That was true. Everything from the past kept trying to haunt me, and I hated it. It just meant that I needed to keep it in the past and not focus on everything that kept being fucked up in our lives.

Only it felt like maybe I was doing this whole looking forward to the future thing wrong.

But what did I know? I was just a guy trying not to be the failed Wilder in business, starting up a company that I was decent at, while not only fucking my employee outside but doing my best to act as if nothing had happened. Oh yes, I was doing great not thinking about the past. I was just fucking up the present repeatedly.

"Okay," I said after a moment, pushing my shitty thoughts out of my brain. "Let's talk wedding. Who's your best man?" I asked Ridge, and Brooks grinned, looking as relieved as I felt by changing the subject.

"I was thinking maybe Eli," Ridge said and laughed. "Or, I don't know, Trace?"

"I don't think so, asshole," I teased.

"Okay, it seems like we're going to have to have some game, or some way to decide who wins."

"We all know Gabe's going to win," Brooks grumbled. "He always wins at stupid games like that."

"Well, then we're just going to have to gang up on

him," I said defiantly, and both my brothers laughed, as we made our way to lunch.

We spoke of wedding plans, and upcoming batches of booze and events, and whatever the hell Brooks was building next.

We made plans for the future and didn't wallow in our pasts.

Because we had to move on. I had to stop making mistakes.

My phone buzzed again, Isabelle sharing another memory, and I had to wonder why my past kept wanting to scream at me when I wanted nothing to do with it.

I had made enough mistakes, especially over the past few days. I didn't need to make any more.

Even though I had a feeling I wasn't going to be so lucky.

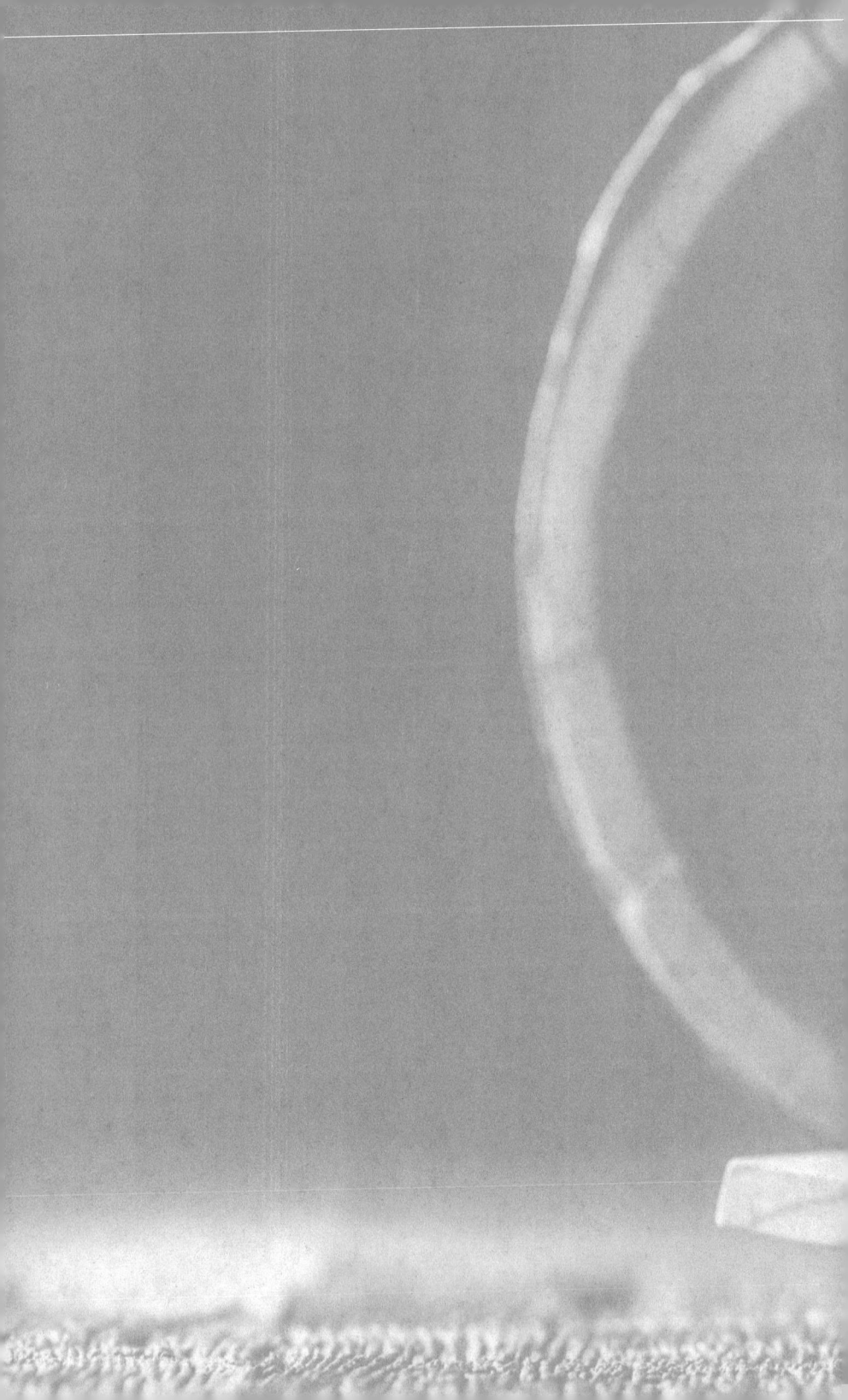

CHAPTER NINE
AVA

I hadn't realized I would be good at this. Maybe I should have. Maybe I should have believed in myself. But that would require you know, believing in myself.

It had taken me far too long into my marriage to realize I needed something beyond what Aaron gave me. I should have stood up for myself long before I had lost part of myself along the way into my marriage.

I had done it to myself, wanting to stay home with Faith as much as possible, and then later, not having the money to go back to school because raising a child took most of our funds. I understood that—what I hadn't understood was that Aaron had been siphoning money for himself, and later, Isabelle. I took odd jobs wherever

I could with just a high school education. I had done my best, and ended up at a diner where I hated every minute of it except that I could be with my child.

But now I was an assistant manager of a bar and distillery, and loving it.

It was so strange. I felt as if I was meant to do this. It was a lot of organizing, thinking outside the box, and working with people who not only liked their jobs but were good at them. And the bartending? It suited my need to be with people. Despite everything, I was still an extrovert. I liked being with people. I liked figuring out exactly what drinks somebody wanted when they said they wanted something sweet or tart, or something with an umbrella. I rolled my eyes at that request, but it was fun figuring out something different for them. I enjoyed working with the staff, with the Wilders, and finding my place.

The hours were different, and I had to rely on others to watch Faith more than I wanted, but Faith was thriving.

"Okay, what about something sweet, but not with pineapple," the woman at the bar said, and I smiled, going through my drink list. I had always been the bartender at parties we'd had at the house. I enjoyed mixing up concoctions. That Wyatt had been the same had led to our rivalry. We had always tried to outdo each other with drinks and different concoctions. I shouldn't have been surprised when that creativity and competitiveness turned into some of the best sex of my life.

I held back a groan, hating myself for letting that come back to my mind. I didn't need to think about him or sex. Again.

Nor me breaking down in his arms. That sounded like a bad deal all around.

"Okay, how about this," I said, after having mixed a watermelon gin drink with a little bit of sparkling wine.

She took a sip and grinned.

"This is perfect."

"I'm glad you like it. It's sort of a different version of a French 75."

"Thank you so much."

I grinned, then went to make another drink before going to the other side of the bar. When Wyatt came up, I swallowed my curse. It was hard to think with him around. Hell, it was hard to do anything these days with him.

But we were doing what we agreed to do—pretend that nothing happened.

But as soon as I met his gaze, I couldn't focus. So perhaps I wasn't as good at this as I thought.

Perhaps I was losing my damn mind.

"Was today good?" Wyatt asked, and I nearly answered with a personal response. But we were just employer and employee right now. He was the owner and operator, and I helped maintain the bar and with any additional paperwork needed. Nothing more, nothing less.

I swore he could see the war going on in my mind, so I just smiled brightly, acting as if I wasn't on a precipice of something I didn't want to think about.

"Doing great. Cassidy is working on the people in the corner, but it's been a reasonable afternoon."

"A lot of guests from the wedding who don't want to drive out to another place or get delivery or eat at a fancier restaurant come here. I think it's been working so far. We've filled a need."

"You really have. You Wilders have it all figured out."

He snorted. "I don't know if that's the case, but we're trying our best. So, you're off for the night?"

I nodded. "As if we weren't the ones that went through the schedule to make that happen."

"What plans do you and Faith have?" he asked, and my stomach did a little twist, because I was thinking about him when I shouldn't.

This was going to be a lot harder than I thought.

"Faith is spending the night with your nieces and nephews."

His eyes widened. "Really?"

"Really. The twins and Eli and Alexis's daughter are all doing a huge cousin sleepover, with Eli in charge," I said, mentioning Wyatt's eldest cousin.

"Eli's going to have four kids underfoot?"

"Yes. And Alexis will help once she gets back because, apparently, she has something going on tonight." I was a little worried at first, mostly because I didn't know if Eli could handle it all, but apparently Evan was going to be there too—another one of Wyatt's cousins.

"That's going to be a sight. So, you don't have anything to do tonight?"

"Um..." I swallowed hard, and before I could wonder what he meant by that, because of course he wasn't asking me for anything, the watermelon French 75 woman waved at me.

"I'm so sorry to interrupt, but I was wondering if I can make a to-go order real quick? I'm sorry," she said, and I just grinned.

"That's what I'm here for. You tell me what you need."

"The really hot bartender over there would be nice," she teased before she took a sip of her water. "I can't believe I just said that. How strong was that drink?"

I laughed. "You've had three sips of your first drink. I think that's just what Wyatt Wilder does."

"Oh, he's a Wilder? I've heard good things about them."

"They're okay," I teased before I took her order.

Wyatt was whistling when I walked back to him, and I glared.

"You did not overhear that."

"Of course not. Although I wish you would sing my praises."

"Never," I said. I wondered if this was flirting or if I was losing my mind.

"I'll finish up the takeout order and make her night," Wyatt said, and I rolled my eyes at him.

"It's okay, I can wait for five more minutes for the end of my shift."

"Ava?"

I turned at the sound of Alexis's voice as she walked towards us, her hand over her swelling belly. She was seriously one of the most adorable pregnant women I had ever seen. When I was pregnant with Faith, I had been far more swollen, had adult acne, rosacea, and heartburn that resulted in a permanent scowl. Oh yes, the gloriousness of being pregnant. I had a glow. And it was sweat.

"Hey there."

"I hear you're off tonight so I'm kidnapping you."

I blinked before looking at Wyatt.

"Did you plan this?" I asked.

He held up both hands in innocence. "Of course not. But I really want to see her kidnap you. Can I watch?" Wyatt asked.

Alexis just rolled her eyes. "Shush, you. You're a menace."

"Of course I am. I'm a Wilder."

With a dramatic sigh she put her hands over her belly. "And I'm growing another. You're all menaces."

"We are. But we love you." He went around the bar to hug her and kissed the top of her head. "Should you be out walking? Do you want to sit?"

"I'm not nearing my due date. I'm fine. I needed the walk."

My eyes widened. "You walked here from the inn?"

"It's not that far, but no, I took the golf cart. Which you will be getting in as well because I'm kidnapping you."

"Oh. I was just going to go home and organize a few things."

My meager possessions. Alone. Because even though I was an extrovert, right then I wanted to be alone.

"I don't think so," Maddie said as she skipped her way in. Maddie was one of the managers of the winery and the wine clubs. I wasn't sure what all she did because she seemed to be in a thousand places at once.

She was married to Elijah Wilder and was also glowing —she had told all of us that she was in her first trimester the day before. The two pregnant women linked arms and scowled at me.

Apparently, I was going to be kidnapped. I could not say no to them.

I wasn't sure how they did that. Did it come with marrying a Wilder? Or did they have that in their repertoire to begin with?

"Seriously. I don't need to be kidnapped. I was just going to go work at the house."

"Your kid is with my kid and my husband. You are going to come have a Wilder girls' night."

"But I'm not a Wilder," I blurted.

Wyatt chuckled beside me as Maddie waved me off. "Psst. Whatever. You don't need to worry about that. We take in people we like all the time. And it is time for a girls' night."

"Why does that sound ominous?"

Wyatt reached around and undid my apron. I had to ignore the way he smelled, and the look the girls gave me.

I cleared my throat and took a step away from him. "I can handle that."

"You were going to stand here like a deer in headlights and be in my way. Go have fun. You deserve it."

"I have things to do."

"Like hanging out with us."

I sighed and knew that there was no way I was not going to do this. I wasn't going to have a choice.

Maybe that was okay.

With one last look at Wyatt, who just laughed at me, I gathered my things, waved at everybody, and headed out.

I was escorted out of the bar and distillery, and found myself in the back of the golf cart, wondering what I'd gotten myself into.

Because it was freezing cold, we were all bundled up, and there was a heating blanket on the cart.

"I love this," I said, patting the blanket.

Maddie looked over her shoulder and smiled over at me. "I know, right? Soon we're going to have to use the covered motorized vehicles like regular people, but I enjoy going the back ways to the winery. It saves time."

"And soon I'm not going to be able to even drive this thing, you know, with the whole pregnant belly."

"I can't wait," Maddie said, putting her hand over her still flat stomach.

I laughed, looking at the two of them. "So between the two of you, there's going to be at least two more Wilders coming soon?" I asked.

"Yes. I'm just having the one. Kendall and Evan were the ones with twins."

"There's going to be a whole bushel of Wilders soon."

"You say that as if it's a bad thing," Maddie said with a laugh.

"It's not, although didn't your husbands have like six siblings?"

"Yep. Eli's parents had seven kids, while Wyatt's parents only had four."

I shuddered. "I can't believe you just said 'only' four."

Maddie laughed. "I know, right? But I don't think any of us are going to try for seven or anything."

"I think you'd run out of space in the state of Texas."

"That is very true," Alexis said with a laugh. She pulled into the reserved parking space behind the winery, and we made our way inside.

"Isn't it a little weird to have a girls' night at a winery when you are both pregnant?"

Maddie shrugged. "I work with wine every day. I lead tastings even though I don't get to taste myself."

"It helps that you have all the experience in the world," Alexis put in.

"I try. And there're other people that can taste the wine for me."

"Anyway, as for girls' night," Maddie continued, "it's what we've always done. And even though we can't have the soft cheeses we used to, Kendall always has snacks for us."

"You're right, I do," Kendall said as she came forward, her beautiful hair flowing down her back. Aurora was beside her, her hands holding a tray filled with sweet temptations.

"Plus, the baker is marrying into the Wilders, so we get even more cake." Maddie winked.

I looked at the women as they all talked over one another, but still seemed to be having conversations that made sense. They were a family, the women who had learned to not tame a Wilder, but be with one.

This wasn't ever going to be me.

This was a glimpse into a family that had been made. They weren't just the wives of the Wilders, they were friends and powerful women all in their own right. And there were two more not here, Bethany and Lark, who would be here for the holidays. They were superstars. But the other women here had their own power as well.

"You know I could barely handle marrying one, I cannot believe you married two," I said to Sidney.

Sidney blushed. "Elliot and Trace work well together. But it helps that they're in love too." That blush of hers told me exactly how much in love the three of them were, and I had to admit I was jealous.

Not of the idea of two men, but for someone that could show their love.

I hadn't realized until it was too late that it wasn't like that with me and Aaron.

But I wasn't going to feel bad right then.

So that's how I found myself with a small glass of champagne, a plate full of appetizers and cakes, and listening as the women of the Wilders made plans for the holidays, future plans for the Wilder Retreat, and gossiped.

Not petty gossip, but the fun kind that was all about family.

"And even though Eliza didn't come for Thanksgiving and can't come for Christmas, she and her brood are coming down for New Year's. So of course we're going to have another party, in addition to the regular holiday one."

"Eliza is Wyatt's cousin?" I asked.

I realized in that moment that I had centered Wyatt in the question, rather than any one of their husbands. I really needed to get my subconscious under control.

The women gave each other looks but didn't pry. Oh, I knew they wanted to, but the gossip wasn't about me...for now.

I would never tell them that Wyatt and I had sex. That would be asking for trouble. Mostly trouble for me, because these women wouldn't be cruel about it. No, they would just want to know how I felt.

And since I did not know how I felt, I wasn't going to bring it up. We wouldn't be doing it again, so there was no need.

"Yes, she's one of the legendary E names," Aurora said with a laugh. "She's great and has two amazing kids and a very hunky husband. He's a Montgomery."

I frowned. "Is that supposed to mean something?" I asked.

"Only if you're in Colorado," Aurora said with a laugh, and squeezed my hand. "There's more of them than Wilders, if you can believe it."

"That really doesn't sound believable."

Everyone laughed, and I took a bite of the pastry cup that Kendall handed over.

"If you're okay with another person in your marriage, Kendall, I think I'm going to have to marry you. Would Evan be okay with that?"

"My husband does not share, but I think a food marriage could be arranged," Kendall said with a laugh.

"Seriously, I'm just going to sit over here in my own bliss." I closed my eyes and moaned at the last bite, and everyone laughed, however, there was some moaning on their ends too.

"So, you have to come to the holiday party," Maddie said, clapping her hands in front of her.

I frowned and looked over at her. "You mean the work party?"

"Well, there's the work party, but then there's the Wilder party. You need to come."

I shook my head. "But that sounds like a family holiday party."

"Yes, but you live on the property. Faith would love it," Alexis said, dragging me in.

"I don't know. I don't want to impose."

"You wouldn't be imposing," Sidney said. "Your mom's not coming in till closer to Christmas, right?" she asked.

I blinked. "How did you know that?"

"Because we have the reservations," Alexis said with a laugh. "And Wyatt mentioned it." She waved it off, and I wondered if I had told him that, or Faith had. I wasn't sure.

I wasn't sure about anything.

"Seriously, please come. We get to wear pretty dresses, and we don't have to be on all the time."

"Oh. Well, maybe. I'll need to ask Faith if she wants to."

"You'll have fun, I promise. No work at all."

As I tentatively agreed, I leaned back, wondering how my life had gotten here.

I was trusting people with my daughter and my future. And it felt right.

And that was why, in no uncertain terms, I could never sleep with Wyatt again.

That would ruin everything.

Even though I had a feeling that I was making a promise I couldn't keep.

Not when I could still feel his touch on me.

CHAPTER TEN

WYATT

GABE:

Why are you wearing a purple sicker on your chin in that photo?

ME:

It's from Faith.

GABE:

That doesn't answer my question.

ME:

Yeah, it does.

GABE:

So a little girl asks you to wear a sticker and you go out in public with it on your face?

GABE:

...

GABE:

> Okay, I just answered my own question. Though why did Faith ask you to wear one? Or is it because she thinks you're pretty with it?

My lips twitched as my younger brother continued to text his thoughts on Faith and purple stickers. The idea that Rockstar Gabe could spend a few moments of free time on the phone with me making fun of me and stickers made me feel like maybe we Wilders were doing something right.

It wasn't always easy when Gabriel was out on tour while people screamed his name and threw themselves at his feet. Though those same people demanded everything short of Gabriel's soul because he was their public commodity—and then some claimed his soul along the way.

In the end, however, he was still a Wilder through and through.

ME:

> You'd wear the sticker on stage at the Grammys in February if Faith asked you, wouldn't you?

GABE:

> I might do it even if she doesn't ask. I'd look a hell of a lot better than you wearing it.

ME:

You're an asshole.

GABE:

I learned from the best. Now, you going to tell me why you're spending so much time with Faith? And don't lie to me and tell me it's because Ava works for you.

I cursed under my breath, grateful we hadn't done a video chat since Gabe could read my face just as well as Brooks and Ridge could. That hadn't always been the case, though of course maybe it had. They'd known I wasn't happy with Isabelle long before I had. I'd just thought marriage was hard and that's how you survived the world as an adult—doing things you didn't understand and forcing yourself to live with the decisions you made when you were a different person.

GABE:

So. You just not going to answer? I see how it is. Let me get into the group chat and find out the details.

ME:

You're an asshole.

GABE:

That's all you have to say? You sound like a broken record.

ME:

I'm going to break your record right now if you don't shut up.

GABE:

Look at you, buying my vinyls like you love me or something. O.B.S.E.S.S.E.D.

ME:

How long did it take you to type that out on your phone?

GABE:

I don't want to talk about it.

GABE:

I'd rather talk about you and Ava.

ME:

makes crunching noise What was that? Sorry. I can't hear you. It sounds like a bad connection.

GABE:

That doesn't work in a text message, dumbass. That's fine though. I'll just go to the group chat without you.

ME:

You have a group chat without me?

GABE:

You know with three brothers, we've all got a group chat with each of us, then with three of the four of us. Mini groups rule the world.

ME:

It's not like that with Ava, she works for me. That's it.

GABE:

Keep lying. But whatever. I need to head to sound check. See you soon. Christmas is going to be lit.

ME:

Never say lit again.

GABE:

Fine. But I might be able to pull it off with that purple sticker. Be safe, fuckface.

ME:

You too, dumbass.

I set down my phone on the desk in my office and sighed. I leaned back in my chair, running my hands over my face, knowing I was screwed. Hell, I'd been screwed long before Gabriel decided to be a nosy jerk. I should have been better at lying to him about Ava, but what the hell was I supposed to say?

Yes, Ava and I slept together.

Or at least, banged against a tree.

But it's not like I could say that. Or let anyone else know. Yet my brothers had seen how awkward I had been around Rory, and then Ava. I'd been a better liar at one point in my life.

Well…before, when I'd lost everything. Only I didn't think about those things. I couldn't.

There was no going back, and I knew that. So why was I even trying?

It wasn't like Ava was ever going to be mine—which I didn't want anyway.

It would be better for all of us if we kept things quiet and we walked away.

"Wyatt?"

I nearly fell out of my desk chair at the sound of Ava's voice at the door and I looked up, breath escaping me.

"Sorry! I knocked on the doorframe, but you were lost in thought. I didn't mean to scare you." She bit her lip, then narrowed her gaze as she studied me. I didn't want to see that though because if I did, then maybe she'd see something that was far better left unsaid and buried.

Ava wasn't mine.

Ava narrowed her eyes. "What are you staring at?"

I cleared my throat, not realizing that I had been staring at her. At her sharp cheekbones, and the way her mouth parted ever so slightly. It was not smart for me to think of Ava in any way other than as my employee. A friend of a friend.

No, that was doing both of us a disservice. She was a friend. But nothing more.

I knew I couldn't have it be anything more. Even thinking about that purple sticker with Faith from the day before was just too much. Because it reminded me of everything that I couldn't have.

Didn't know why I would be surprised about that.

"Anyway, I finished the paperwork that you needed last night, and now I'm having trouble with the kegs."

I quickly got up, pushing away all random thoughts that had nothing to do with the situation.

"Yeah, I'll help. Which one is it?"

"The Shiner."

I rolled my eyes. "It's always the fucking Shiner. It doesn't matter that I move it around, it's always the Shiner."

"Is that all bars, or just yours?"

"Just this one so far. I never had this problem with the Shiner at the place up north, but there it was another beer. There's just always one troublemaker."

"Good to know. It's been a while since I did this. I usually had problems with people stealing my decaf pots and putting regular in them."

"Well, that just sounds like a lawsuit. People drink decaf for a reason."

"Tell me about it. I am grateful that I don't need to deal with that crowd anymore. Of course, now I have this horrible feeling that one day they're going to show up here, and I'm going to be serving that annoying sleazeball guy who always wanted his eggs sunny side up so they look like breasts and would mention that to me every time."

"Well, if that happens, tell Sam and he'll kick his ass."

She rolled her eyes, considering Sam would probably break down if he had to beat up somebody. He was like a hundred pounds soaking wet, all wiry, not a lick of muscle.

"I really do like working with Sam. He's great at what he does. I didn't know so much went into creating a product. I've never been on that side of it."

"I went to business school with extra classes so I could do this, but I didn't think I'd be here either. Sam though? He's the real genius. I'm just the one with the hope and a plan and some family to help."

"Don't put yourself down for that. You do well." She scowled again. "Sometimes. Sometimes you're just an ass."

"Thank you for putting me in my place. Though I am your boss. You probably should treat me better."

"No, I don't think I will," she said with a laugh as she put on a bright smile and went to go help a guest. I went to go fix the keg again, annoyed with the damn thing. The thing was cursed. Just like I was. Maybe that's why I liked Shiner Bock so much.

We went back to work as I ignored my paperwork

and sat behind the bar with Ava, keeping things going. We had a late rush, and I was grateful for it. Being in the black when it came to any business was a cause for celebration. The fact that people seemed to like coming back for the food and ambiance just made it even better. We had additional security, new locks, and cameras. Nobody had really noticed it though, they felt safe when they were in here anyway. We hadn't publicized the break-in, although it had hit the crime circuits so some people knew. But we were honest about it. Yes, I had gotten my ass beat, and yes, they had stolen money, but we were doing our best to keep people safe. And nobody seemed to feel as if they weren't.

But it did mean that nobody was allowed to close alone anymore.

Of course, Ava and I would be closing together, as Faith was spending the night at her Aunt Rory's house for a girls' night, and the rest of the staff had opened. So it would be just me and Ava cleaning up.

We could handle that. We were adults.

Nothing else needed to happen.

We had sex once, she had broken down in my arms, and I had been reminded of why I didn't want any future with her.

There were other reasons, ones that had nothing to do with the fact that she worked with me, and everything to do with her past and mine.

It would be better for everybody if I kept her off my mind.

"Hey, Wyatt," a familiar voice said, and I turned to see one of our regulars waving me down from their table in the corner. I picked up two drinks from the end of the bar and made my way to the table next to the regular, handing off the drink with a smile, before going to the man who had been one of the first people through the doors and had been a constant source of laughter since.

"I see you're here making sure the walls stay up. I appreciate it. Can I get you guys anything?" I asked.

"No, no, you're doing great. We're about to cash out since it's near closing. But I just wanted to say, that new hire? She's amazing."

It took all within me not to turn to Ava at his words. Because once I did, something was going to happen. Jeff, the man who could read me decently well, would see something in my eyes I'd rather him not, or Ava would notice. I had to be better than that. Because there was no future for us, not just because I was her boss.

"Yeah? That's good to hear."

"Much better than that last one. Don't get me wrong, the lady was nice. But she would rather sit at the bar and talk to whoever was around than get any work done."

I frowned at Jeff. "Why didn't you tell me you didn't like the old assistant manager?"

"Like you wanted me in your business." The old man guffawed.

That made me roll my eyes.

"Oh, so you can be in my business now?"

"That's my prerogative as an elderly retired man."

"If you were elderly and retired, thinking that you are of the age to make shit up like that, then just prepare me for the end of days," I said with a laugh.

"Anyway, I'm an old man who likes this Ava. Don't let her get away." He gave me a pointed look, and I just shook my head.

"She's good for the business. Of course I'm not going to let her get away."

"You know that's not what I was saying."

"And you know that that's all there is. I'm allowed to have a woman work for me and not need her like that. You know that, Jeff."

I was literally lying to myself and him at this point, but I didn't care.

Jeff gave me a sad look, as if I was missing out on one of the most crucial things in the world, before I laughed and went to help the next table. Ava and I worked alongside each other quickly, nodding and speaking to one another when we had to, and it felt right. Easy. Like there wasn't any tension or awkwardness between us. This could totally work. Maybe I hadn't fucked up everything.

By the time we were the only two left in the building, I was tired, but still had more paperwork to do that night.

"Are you going to need help with all those?" Ava asked, gesturing towards the stack of receipts and other paperwork that always accumulated by the end of the day.

"No, I've got it. I don't have to do most of this tonight. But I do want to double-check a few things."

"No problem. It's nice not feeling rushed since I don't have Faith waiting for me at home."

I looked up at her then and frowned. "Are you okay about that? I mean, you could leave right now and go to Rory's house."

She gave me a look. "And leave you alone? Even though the rules are we don't leave anybody alone here, especially with what happened to you?"

I winced. We were alone in my office, the front door double-locked and all the security on.

"Fine then, take a seat. I should be done soon so you don't have to wait too long."

Ava gave me a look, then pulled out her phone before taking a seat on the side of the desk.

"It's late, is Faith sleeping?" I asked, despite myself.

Ava looked up at me and nodded. "Yes, I'm just

looking at photos that Rory sent throughout the night." She turned the phone so I could see Faith upside down on the back of the couch, mouth in a big grin. It looked like she was laughing and crying at the same time.

"That's a lot of energy."

"I know, right? She told me that she gave you one of her favorite stickers. Because apparently you helped make sure she could meet the chickens."

I shrugged, my attention on my paperwork. Or at least that's what I told myself.

"Yes, but I've already gotten shit for the sticker."

"From who?"

"Gabe," I grumbled.

"How did Gabe know that you had the sticker?"

"Because it might have been on my chin on a photo that I forgot about."

"Oh, I'm going to need to see that."

She reached for my phone and I pulled it out of her reach.

"You don't need to see."

"Come on. The big bad Wilder with a cute little sticker on his face is something I need to see."

"You're a menace," I grumbled, before unlocking the phone so she could look through my photos.

She had her feet up and was scrolling through them, when I realized that I had literally just let her look through all my photos without even thinking about it.

"You know, I could have porn in there."

Ava looked up from my phone and raised a brow.

"Unless I'm about to see some other woman's tits, it's fine. I've seen your boobs before." She froze. "Oh my God, is Isabelle in here?" She shuddered and threw my phone at me.

I growled and caught the phone.

"No. I don't take naked photos of people."

"And they've never sent them to you?"

I shrugged. "Maybe. But if I'm not currently sleeping with them, I'm not going to keep their photos. Call it a point of pride, but I'm not going to ever risk my phone being hacked and nude photos getting leaked and then suddenly I have revenge porn."

Ava winced. "Oh, that would suck. I never sent photos to anyone. Even when I was sleeping with them. Well, not that there were many people because I started dating Aaron so young. But still."

I was not going to think about how many people she had slept with or not.

Thankfully Ava changed the subject to discuss a distributor change, and we talked about business for a little bit before I got up to file something. Only I hadn't realized Ava had done the same thing and our bodies brushed against each other. I nearly knocked her over and reached out and gripped her hips instinctively, keeping her steady. She reached out and gripped my shoulders.

She swallowed hard and looked down between us.

"Sorry."

"No problem. Of course, I think I'm the one that knocked you over."

"Yeah. Maybe."

"We should get going. It's late."

"You're right. It is late."

"And even though Faith isn't there to greet you when you get home, you should still get home."

"You're right. We both should get home." She paused. "Separately. To our own homes."

My gaze caught on her mouth, watching the way her tongue licked her lips.

"Yeah. That's exactly what we should do."

And then my mouth was on hers, making another big fucking mistake.

I pulled her hips towards mine, so she could feel the hard length of my erection against her stomach. She groaned into my mouth, tugging on my shirt.

I didn't think, I just pulled her up by her hips and pressed her back against the filing cabinet. It probably wasn't comfortable but she didn't seem to care, because she wrapped her legs around my waist. I slid my hand up her side, cupping her breast underneath her shirt, and she arched her back, pressing her body into me.

"I need you," I growled into her mouth, and she nodded.

"Too many clothes," she rasped.

I tugged her shirt over her head, her breasts bouncing just enough that it made me groan. She was so luscious, so full, and I wanted to fuck those tits. But first, I needed to see them. So I pulled down her bra, not caring that it was still on, and lowered my face to her nipple, sucking the pearl between my teeth.

She let out a shocked gasp as I bit down, loving the way her nipples tightened into hard points.

She writhed in my hold, and we both were wearing far too many clothes. So I pulled back, letting her feet fall to the ground before I kissed her again, then pulling my shirt over my head.

Her mouth went to my nipples, sucking on them, as I ran my hands through her hair.

She cupped me over my jeans, rubbing me, and nearly sending me over the edge.

"Wyatt," she gasped.

"I've got you."

And then I went to my knees, undoing the button of her jeans. I shoved them down her legs, pulling off her shoes, baring her in front of me, looking so fucking beautiful it was hard for me to breathe.

"Hop up on the desk."

"This is so stupid."

"Completely."

But she did as I said, and then my face was between her legs, my tongue on that sweet wet pussy of hers.

She threw her head back and screamed something non-intelligible. She tasted of sweetness and a little bit tart. It was all I could do not to pull back and shove my cock deep inside of her just to watch her spasm around me, but I needed her to come first. I needed her to flow on my tongue and fuck my face. And when she began to roll her hips, I was one happy man. I licked and sucked at that sweet, gorgeous cunt, and then she was whispering something, her body more frantic, and when she came, she gushed on my tongue, and I nearly came in my jeans.

Before she could come down off her high, I stood up, unable to hold on any longer. I practically ripped the zipper off my jeans as I shoved them down my hips and took her by her thighs.

"I'm going to fuck you hard. Are you ready?"

"Mm-hmm," she sort of mumbled but she nodded, so I took it as a yes. I flipped her on her stomach, ass in the air, her toes not even touching the ground as I kept her steady. Papers flew to the ground, and the computer monitor nearly followed, but I didn't give a fuck. She gripped the edge of the desk, and then I was shoving deep inside her. She was wet, hot, and her cunt was still fluttering from her orgasm. She tightened around my shaft, and I moved hard and fast, needing her. My balls tightened, ready to release, and I held on, needing her. She met me thrust for thrust once I let her feet touch the ground, and then I moved her up again, needing to be the one in control. She had her head down, ass up, and it was the most beautiful thing I'd ever seen, the long lines of her back looking like an invitation. So I leaned over and licked the sweat off her back, needing that saltiness.

"Come. Come for me. Feel my cock deep inside you."

"Wyatt."

"That's it. Say my name. Tell me who's fucking you."

"You are, Wyatt. You are."

"That's it. That's it."

I gripped her ass with a bruising force, and then I was coming along with her, her cunt gripping my dick as I filled her, my orgasm coming full force.

I roared her name, both of us shaking as I finally came down, needing to catch my breath.

I moved on top of her, trying to breathe, even as my hips continued a steady and soft roll, still pumping in and out of her.

I kissed her shoulder, then her neck, just needing her taste, her touch.

"We didn't use a condom," she whispered, and I nodded.

"I would say fuck, but I haven't been keeping condoms on me because I didn't want to presume."

"Maybe we should do better." She paused and I slid out of her, using a napkin to clean us both up. It was sticky, hot, and I didn't know what I was supposed to say.

The awkwardness of what had just happened settled in.

"So," she said, as we shifted so we could get dressed. "That was just a pressure release."

"Totally. We didn't ask for that. But it happened. We're not going to ignore it because when we ignore it, we just make it a big deal."

Ava nodded. "You're right. It happened because we're good at it. But it doesn't have to be a thing. Neither one of us has time for a thing."

I nodded, then held out my hand.

She looked down at it and smirked before reaching forward to give it a shake.

"Good. I'm going to go to the bathroom to clean up, and then we can head to each of our homes. Separately. And we don't have to talk about this again."

"No problem."

And then she walked away, leaving me standing there, knowing that this being a pressure release or whatever the fuck you wanted to call it was a good label. Because it didn't matter that there was chemistry between us.

Getting together would just screw things up.

She had to go home, to where she lived with her kid. I wasn't about to get in the middle of a ready-made family.

I slid my hand over my heart, ignoring the ache there. Ignoring the sharp pains that I always got when thinking about Faith.

Because my kid would've been older than her at this point. My kid hadn't even had a chance.

I had lost it all before I'd even had it. And when I tried to love again, I'd lost the wife I thought I had wanted too.

So I wasn't going to go through any of that again.

I had lost a child before I ever had a chance to meet them, and that was when I told myself I would never be a father. And Isabelle had been fine with that.

But Ava? Even without all the other complications that brought us together and pulled us apart, Faith would always be there. And in telling myself I would be okay with a child now, that meant I would be ignoring what I had vowed to the child I lost before. And I wasn't quite sure how I could rectify that, even if others did every fucking day.

When Ava came out of the bathroom and gave me a

look, trying to smile as if nothing had happened, I did the same right back.

We would head home and we wouldn't talk about this. Even if we ended up in bed or outdoors or in an office again, that would be all it was.

Hot sex, a pressure release, friends with benefits, or whatever else she wanted to call it.

There couldn't be a future. Not with the promise I had made as an eighteen-year-old kid.

So I would lean into that pain and that promise.

Because it was the only thing keeping me where I was.

CHAPTER ELEVEN
AVA

"**M**om! Are we wearing the purple sparkling dresses together?"

I winced at Faith's shout from the other side of the cabin but didn't scold her for yelling since I was currently standing in my leggings and crop top in front of my open closet while Faith was in her room.

Trying to choose something to wear to a family party for a family that wasn't your own while not having many clothes because your ex-husband took most of them out of spite didn't make for a stress-free evening.

In fact, I could really use something to calm myself.

Like perhaps a martini.

Or a quick jump in a frozen lake.

"I don't *have* the purple sparkling dress, baby."

Aaron had taken that from me too—not that I'd tell Faith that. Of course, she was eight and far too smart for her own good. So perhaps she already had an inkling of what happened, but I wasn't about to get into that.

Tonight was about inserting ourselves into the lives of the Wilders and pretending that this wasn't a bad idea ready to explode in our faces. I hadn't even told Wyatt about the invitation from the Wilder women. I should have, of course. That might have made it easier to run away. Or made things not be so...sticky.

But after the night in his office where I'd lost my damn mind and had yet again one of the best orgasms of my life, I hadn't been able to face him alone.

Thankfully work and spending time with Faith had taken all my time these past two days. But I'd be going to his family party where he was probably expecting to just hang out with those close to him and not a woman he kept accidentally fucking in random places around his property.

The sound of feet padding along the floor hit my ears as Faith ran into the bedroom and wrapped her arms around my waist.

"I'm sorry, I forgot. Do you have another sparkly dress?"

I shook my head. "No, baby, I don't. But I have cute pants and a sparkly top. What do you think about that?"

"It's not purple," she said as I pointed to the silver sparkly top that I could make into a holiday outfit. It looked more suited for New Year's than it did for Christmas or any of the other winter holidays the Wilders might be celebrating, but I would make it work.

I wrapped my arms around my little girl and rubbed my hands over her shoulders. She sighed happily, resting her head on my body. That's when I realized she was so much taller than she had been. My baby was growing up.

"I'll wear enough purple for us both."

I laughed, shaking my head. "What is with this purple phase? You used to love green."

"I still love green. But I just felt like purple. But I have that dress, remember?"

I nodded, since I had bought the purple dress for her.

The fact that I now had medical insurance, and enough of an income that I had a meager savings account, meant the world to me. No matter what happened between me and the Wilders in the future, I would never forget what they had done for us. When Wyatt and the others had taken me in and helped me protect my little girl.

That was why messing around with Wyatt was a problem.

A very bad problem.

I shook myself from that and patted my daughter's back. "Okay, we need to leave soon, so I'm going to see if this shirt works."

"You'll be beautiful no matter what, Mom. And I think it'll work."

"While I think you're a bit biased, I'm going to take the compliment."

"Of course. Because I'm always right."

I rolled my eyes at that, even though she was right more often than not. That was going to be a little scary once she became an adult.

Oh God, or a *teenager*.

But that was fine. I was excited for those teenage years because we'd have each other.

I wasn't going to be one of those moms that cried every single time she thought about her daughter growing up. That would just be ridiculous. So, why was I tearing up right now?

I shoved those thoughts to the side since they weren't going to help anyone and quickly got dressed. We weren't necessarily running late, but we would be if I stewed in my own thoughts and self-pity any longer than I already had.

I didn't have time for self-pity when I had to go to a party with the Wilders.

I quickly put my hair in some form of updo with bobby pins that I would probably take out later. I had put soft curls in and wanted to try something new, but it didn't feel like I was doing it right.

When the doorbell rang, I frowned. We weren't expecting anyone, as we had to head over to the main house soon.

"I've got it."

"Faith, you know the rules."

"But I know who it is."

Frowning, I put in my final earring as I walked through the small living room and nearly tripped over my own feet.

Wyatt stood there wearing a gray button-down tucked into darker gray slacks, with his sleeves folded up to show off his forearms.

Damn it. I really liked those forearms. There had to be something wrong with me for even daring to think that.

"Wyatt? Are you going to the party too?"

I held back a wince at that because I hadn't thought Wyatt knew we were going, and of course he was going, it was his family party, after all.

Wyatt held out his arm as Faith hugged him, and I ignored that little clutch in my chest.

I had to protect my daughter. But Wyatt was safe, at least when it came to Faith. He was kind, and so attentive. They were friends. The Wilders treated everyone with respect and care.

And I needed to make sure that my heart understood the difference, along with my brain.

Only I didn't really feel like I was making sense at all.

"I am," he said, squeezing Faith's shoulder. "And there's been a change of location, so I figured I'd pick you up."

I frowned and reached for my phone.

"Crap, I didn't realize I missed a call. And text."

"We had a last-minute power issue thanks to the city, which doesn't affect the guests but means that we're moving the party to Eli and Alexis's place. It is just down the road, just off the Wilder property."

"For some reason I thought you guys all lived in this little cool compound together," I teased, trying to make sure the plans that I had for escaping with Faith early if needed could still happen.

I felt like he was on to me though, so I just smiled a little brittlely.

"Is everyone okay?" I asked.

"Of course. Naomi and Amos and the rest of the crew are here with the guests, so we Wilders are going to party."

"Can I party too?" Faith asked, and Wyatt beamed.

"Of course. I'm here to pick you guys up because while there's tons of parking at my cousin's place, there isn't enough for all one hundred cars we might need. So you guys are going to head over with me. Hope that's okay. You didn't answer your texts, so I sort of just made the decision for us."

"Oh. Well." I really wish I would've been checking my phone instead of getting lost in my thoughts, because I didn't know if there was any way out of this.

"Let me get my bag," Faith said as she ran past me to get her small beaded bag.

"You have a purse?" Wyatt asked, the grin on his face huge. "I didn't know you were old enough to have a purse."

Faith did that lovely roll of her eyes again that I knew I should squash, but honestly she wasn't being too disrespectful, as Wyatt was just teasing her.

"I don't use it all the time. But Mom said I could have it for tonight because it's a party and I want to be sparkly." Faith twirled in her purple dress, and I quickly snapped a few photos with my phone, the phone that was never going to leave my hands again.

"You look beautiful. Like a princess." Wyatt took Faith's hand and bowed deeply.

"You're being silly," Faith said, but she was smiling, her heart in her eyes.

Damn it.

"Well, my ladies, do you have everything you need? I hear there are cheese balls and meatballs and every type of appetizer you could ever want at this party. My cousin's wife has been cooking up a storm."

"I love Ms. Kendall's food. She's the best cook." Faith put her hand over her mouth to mock whisper. "Even better than Mom."

"I heard that, but I agree."

"Well, you can't really compete with Kendall when it comes to food. My future sister-in-law Aurora? She can out-bake us all."

"You are very lucky with your family," I said with a smile.

"Yeah, I am."

He met my gaze, and I wondered what he was thinking. Or maybe I didn't. Maybe if I just breathed, we would be safe.

"Are you sure you're going to be able to bring us home?" I asked, feeling awkward.

He smiled at me. "Yes. I'm not drinking tonight, because I am the designated driver for the two most beautiful women at the party."

"You're funny," Faith said, and this time I mimicked her by rolling my eyes.

"Are you sure you want to say that with your family members being the other women there?"

"I said what I said. Seriously though, it's not a big deal."

"I wasn't sure how long we were going to stay."

He gave me a look that spoke volumes, but I kept my gaze steady.

"Then when you are ready, we come home. It's not too far of a drive. Let's go. If you're ready."

"I'm ready."

I looked at my daughter, and then at Wyatt, and knew I was outnumbered.

I wasn't sure I liked that.

I grabbed my bag, made sure everything was unplugged that needed to be, and then somehow I was in the passenger seat of his SUV, with Faith in the back chirping about something she had seen out with Rory the day before. We had moved the booster from my car to his, though Faith was just at the legal limit. Anyone below eight in the state of Texas needed a booster seat, and she was right at the height level where she could get away without it, but we were used to it.

Just another way to show me that things kept changing.

And I needed to change with them.

We pulled into the driveway of a beautiful home that was set against a large hill with trees all around, and it took my breath away.

"Those oak trees are beautiful."

"I know, right? The builder wanted to tear them down to make it easier for his guys to get some of the construction done, but Eli made them build another road in on the backend. It was a whole thing, but it didn't destroy any old trees, and when my brother came out to check on it, since he's a builder too, he did all the finishing touches."

"The talent in your family is immense."

"Thank you for calling me talented," he said with a wink.

I laughed. "I said your family. But sure."

"Can I get out now, Mom?" Faith asked.

"You know it. Come on, I'll help you out."

"I've got it."

And then my baby girl who didn't feel like such a baby anymore jumped out of the car, beaded bag in hand, before running to Alexis and Eli's daughter Kylie.

Kylie was much younger, as were Reese and Cassie, but the four of them seem to be fast friends.

"Well, it seems I'm not needed," I said with a laugh.

Wyatt brushed his hand along mine, sending chills down my spine.

"You're needed. Come on, they'll be safe inside, and I hear pigs in a blanket calling my name."

"You really think she's going to have pigs in a blanket? So classy."

"I asked for them specifically. And Kendall never disappoints."

"You know I don't," Kendall said as she pointed us towards the table when we walked in.

"Your little pigs in their little blankets are resting comfortably. And yes, I used the tube dough, even though it literally broke me. But I understand that the preservatives are close to your heart, so I'll let you keep those. Just know I will never use tube dough again, unless it's for a family event."

"I love you," Wyatt said as he leaned down and brushed a kiss on her cheek.

Kendall just snorted.

"You always say that about my food."

"Get your hands off my woman." Evan came forward and wrapped his arm around Kendall's waist before lifting his chin at me.

"Hey there. Glad you got the message. Sorry for the change in venue."

"I'm just honored to be invited. I know this is a family thing."

"It is, but we like you being here. You're just going to have to deal with us," Kendall said with a laugh.

"Come on, are you in the mood to drink? We also have sparkling cider if you prefer that."

"And I'm making cocktails and mocktails," Lark Thornbird said from the other side of the room, which reminded me that there was a Grammy winner, an Oscar winner, an Emmy winner and most likely a future Tony winner in this room between Bethany and Lark. I was not going to get starstruck, but it was close.

"That sparkling cider sounds good. I feel like I need to keep my wits around me when it comes to you Wilders," I said with a laugh.

"Truer words have never been spoken," Kendall said, and Wyatt just gave me a look.

"What?"

"I feel like I should be offended you need to keep your wits about you around me."

I narrowed my gaze at him.

"Always, Wyatt. Always."

I hadn't meant to say that so softly, or to meet his gaze as intensely, but then someone cleared their throat, and I turned to see Brooks standing there with two glasses in his hand.

"Non-alcoholic sparkling wine, or whatever this is called, for you both. I'm going to go get the real stuff."

"Thank you," I said, taking the glass from him and quickly sidestepping Wyatt.

He was a very dangerous man, and I needed to remember that.

Brooks looked between us but didn't say anything. This wasn't awkward at all.

"By the way, are you ready for that event?" Brooks asked as I took a sip of my fake champagne.

"Yeah, I'm not in the mood to go though. It's going to be a lot of pretending that I care about these people."

"What event?" I asked.

"You didn't tell her?" Brooks asked as Ridge came over with two glasses in his hand, handing one to Brooks.

"This is some form of berry and rosemary concoction that Lark made, all with the Wilder vodka of course. So be nice, or Everett will kick our ass for being mean to her."

I laughed at that but smiled at the cocktails.

"They look pretty."

The guys each took a sip and nodded. "Taste good," they said simultaneously, before snorting.

"So, what's this event?" I asked, trying not to notice the heat of Wyatt at my side.

"It's just a distillery event a couple of hours away. A bunch of the local places get together and hobnob and try to get either more investors, or to get into stores, or to lie about who's better. It sucks."

"Why do you go?"

Wyatt shrugged. "It's just part of the job. I don't usually go to these things, Giselle did, and that was the one thing she was good at."

I cringed at the sound of the woman who once had my job. "So that's why you kept her on?" I paused. "Sorry. None of my business."

"No, that was part of it. And just because it was easier. Though hiring you was the best thing I've ever done."

He quickly took a sip of his drink, as if he was unsure why he'd even said that, and his brothers gave him a look.

"You should go," Ridge put in, an odd expression on his face.

"Me? I don't even know where it is or what it is."

"But you could learn. It's good management skills."

"I'm just learning what those are," I said carefully. "And if it's that far away, I can't leave Faith overnight."

Wyatt cleared his throat. "You should. Come with me."

I turned to him as his brothers slowly backed away, leaving us alone. I didn't know if this was planned, or if the brothers knew there was something sizzling that they wanted to get out of the way of.

But though I heard my daughter's laughter on the other side of the room, and everyone milling about, it felt as if I was alone with Wyatt.

"What?"

"Come with me."

"What?"

"It's not an overnight. The event is mostly during the afternoon, and it's only about two hours away. We can be home by nine o'clock so you can still tuck your daughter in."

"Her bedtime is eight," I said dryly.

"Then you can tuck her in again. I made it sound

like a drag, but it's not that bad. You get to meet people in the business, learn a few things, and you're good at your job. Getting out of the house is good. A Wilder will watch Faith for the day, and it's just a quick event."

"What are you doing, Wyatt?" I asked, aware that others were watching, and that we had started to move closer together.

"Come with me. Let me show you off."

"Like I'm a prized possession?" I asked, my teeth gritted.

"Like you're damn good at your job and that you can learn more things. So when you finally leave to do whatever you want to do rather than what you are forced to do, you'll have the skills."

I didn't know if he was trying to convince me or him with that, but maybe I would go.

Maybe.

"Mom!" Faith said as she came forward. "What are you drinking?" she asked.

"Something you can have," I teased, handing her the glass.

Faith took a sip, her eyes widening. "It's sparkly. I like it."

"Then let's get you a drink," Wyatt said, gesturing towards the bar area. "And then I heard there might be cheese and pastry cups."

"And pigs in a blanket. I love pigs in a blanket."

And without looking back, Wyatt and Faith went hand in hand to the food and beverage area, leaving me behind holding a half-empty glass, wondering what the hell just happened.

Did his family know we had slept together? No. They couldn't, could they?

Maybe. It wouldn't be any of their business, but with a family as close-knit as this, secrets were hard to keep.

That just meant I had to be stronger. Had to be smarter.

Because when it came to Wyatt Wilder, I lost all sense of reality and control.

So I drained the last of my drink, wishing it was actual alcohol, but I didn't move forward. I just watched Wyatt and my daughter laugh together, piling food on their shared plate.

I couldn't mess this up. Not again.

Only, I had a feeling I was falling for a Wilder.

And that was going to be the worst mistake I had ever made. Because there'd be no bouncing back from that, not for Faith.

And not for me.

CHAPTER TWELVE
WYATT

"I don't understand why there is a corporate event three days before Christmas."

"Five days before Christmas Eve," I corrected, my hands white knuckling the steering wheel. It rarely snowed in South Texas; we usually got more ice. Most of us had PTSD from the last ice storm which knocked out the power for the entire state for days at a time. We tried not to think about those times, even though we prepped for it. At least what we could do as a business.

It was cold and raining, but it wasn't icy or snowing. The forecast didn't predict that, but Texas weather was anything but predictable.

"I have no idea. I think they're calling this their own holiday party. And the only reason we're going is because of Jackson Morose."

"Why is that such a scary name?" she asked with a laugh.

I snorted. "I know, right? But he is the guy you talk to in order to get into local stores before you go national. We're already in a few stores, as well as bars and other places that people who know the Wilders frequent. However, we want to reach the whole state of Texas."

"And considering the state of Texas is bigger than all of New England, that's kind of big."

"Scary, isn't it? How big this state is. Considering everyone keeps saying we're just driving down the road a bit to this event, and it's still two hours away."

Ava tapped her fingers on her knee. "I still can't believe I'm coming with you. During my child's Christmas break, and two days before my mother arrives."

"Are you excited to see your mom?" I asked, getting off the highway to make our way down the farm road where the event was taking place.

"I am. It's been forever since she's seen Faith. Video chat and texting are amazing, and we're even handwriting letters even though those take forever to get to and from Canada, but it's totally worth it."

"I know how you feel. It was great and all texting and calling my brothers, but it's not the same."

"Your parents live up north, right?" she asked, and I nodded.

"Yep. But they are going on a cruise this year, which is great because they never actually take vacations for themselves."

"A Christmas cruise?"

"Yeah, apparently a lot of people do it. You don't have to plan anything, and you get good food and booze. I don't know if I could do it, but they're in the Caribbean for the winter, and we keep getting emails and texts of them looking happy."

"But it sucks that they're not here," she said softly.

"Yeah, but they deserve this time. While they do consider my cousins' kids their grandkids, technically they're not grandparents yet." I let my voice trail at that because I remembered what could have been. For more than one of us. But I didn't want to think about that. I couldn't.

I swallowed hard and pushed down those emotions that weren't going to do anybody any good.

"You just said that your parents think of your cousins' kids as grandkids. That makes them grandparents. Believe me, you take whatever grandparents you can get. Faith only has Mom. My mom."

"Because Aaron's parents are dumbasses?" I asked.

"Like father and mother, like son. I just don't want to talk about them right now."

"They haven't called or anything?"

"I don't even know if they know where their grand-daughter lives right now. But there's literally nothing I can do because I'm not going to beg them to love my daughter."

"You shouldn't have to. Though I really want to kick Aaron's ass. Please let me."

I met her gaze, and she shook her head. "No. It's not worth it." She let out a breath. "Speaking of kicking ass, did they ever find out who attacked you?"

That made me laugh, which was odd because I didn't think I'd ever laugh about that.

"That segue hurt. I'm in physical pain right now."

"We both know I'm not good at conversation."

"You are amazing at conversation, you just like to needle me. However, no, they haven't. They're still looking for that rancher, Zach Green. But he's long gone."

"Do you think it was him?"

"A man that was down on his luck and needed help? Maybe. But I don't know. There's been a few robberies around the area, but that comes with business and the holiday season when people are desperate or greedy. I don't know if it was him or someone else. Either way though, we're just trying to move on."

"I'm sorry for bringing it up."

"No, it's okay. I put your safety at risk by not

knowing who did that. If they could take me out, they could do the same to you." I growled out the last words, and she sighed.

"I feel like that is you holding onto the patriarchy and some toxic masculinity issues, but I'm going to let that go."

"No, it's because I can fight, and box, and you can't. You could kick my ass, but that's just because I'd let you."

"Okay. I feel like we need to test that out, but not in front of Faith. I don't want her to think violence is an answer."

"So you're saying you want to wrestle in private?" I teased, then cursed. "Sorry."

"No, it's okay. We're friends, right? We're allowed to make jokes like that. I think." She ran her hands over her face. "Are we almost there yet?"

"GPS says .2 miles until this turn and then we should be there."

"So you need me to schmooze so we can get a deal, and then head back early so I can hug my baby?"

"You're on. The sooner we talk to this guy, the sooner we can be home. We shouldn't have done this."

"What, go to this together?"

Yes, but I didn't say that out loud.

"More like we shouldn't have even done this at all. It's probably just a waste of time."

"Well, if you're going into it thinking that, then of course it's going to be a waste of time. Come on, let's go kick ass and then go home to my baby."

"Sounds like a plan."

"HONESTLY, THAT WAS THE FASTEST I'VE EVER seen that man part with money," I said with a laugh.

Ava joined me laughing. "Well, it helped that he was looking at my boobs the entire time."

I growled at that, a little annoyed, but Ava waved it off.

"I'm kidding. Okay, he somewhat looked at my boobs. But he was also paying attention to what we were saying. The Wilders make a damn good product, and you have great labeling, and everyone just really likes you guys. It helps that you have a foothold in the wine industry, the wedding industry, the hospitality industry, and what else?"

"Well, we have a couple rock stars and actresses and starlets in our wheelhouse as well."

"I always forget that *the* Gabriel Wilder is your brother."

"Excuse me?" I asked, turning up the windshield wipers as the rain started to come down a bit harder.

The storm had come out of nowhere, which annoyed

us to no end considering the forecast hadn't called for it. Only it was getting cold enough that I was afraid it wasn't going to be rain for much longer.

Because the South wasn't prepared for weather like this. And if it started snowing, it wasn't going to be safe to keep going.

And that was something better left not spoken out loud.

"Really? You have a crush on Gabe?"

I didn't know what I was doing. She was off limits. I didn't have a right to be jealous or territorial over the fact that she might find my rock star brother attractive.

"Yes. I mean, I did have a poster on my wall at the apartment. You know, the one that I shared with my daughter." She rolled her eyes at me just like Faith did. "I love your brother's music. I just find it so fascinating that you guys are all brothers. You guys are completely different, and yet all growly possessive at the same time."

I relaxed. "We can't help it. We act like our dad."

"Your poor mom."

"True. She did have to deal with us. However, it could have been worse."

"She could have had seven kids rather than four?" she asked.

"Exactly. So anyway, is your mom coming in tomorrow or the day after?" I asked, as I made sure my lights were on high, the rain turning to sleet and getting harder to see through.

"She is supposed to be here tomorrow. I'm waiting on a text from her, but with this storm, and the service being so spotty, I'm a little worried." She paused for a second. "Are you okay? Are you good driving?"

"I'm going to be honest, this fucking sucks. I'm pretty sure that it's ice on the road."

"Wyatt."

"It's fine. I'm driving slowly and as safely as I can, but I can't say the same about the people around us though."

"How much longer?"

We both glanced at the GPS, but my gaze went right back to the icy road in front of me. "It should be an hour, but at this rate I don't know."

"It's okay. Just go slow. I'll try to text the crew and let them know we're on our way, but we're delayed."

"Do you have service?"

"No," she said, her voice tight.

"Faith is fine. I'd be more worried about us."

"Totally not helping," she said, and I gripped the steering wheel harder, and cursed as the car in front of us began to spin.

"Hold on, Ava!" I called out as we reached the same patch of black ice before I could stop and I spun into the skid as well. We spun twice, headlights filling our vision as we faced oncoming traffic before finally righting ourselves in the middle of the road.

Everybody started honking their horns, but I pulled onto the shoulder and stopped, my hands shaking as I looked over at Ava.

"Are you okay? Are you hurt?"

"I'm fine. Are you okay? You did so well with that. I don't think I would've been able to swerve into that skid like that."

"I have practice driving up north. Hell, I don't think it's safe for us to go much further."

"Well, it's not safe for us to stay in a car. How much gas do you have?"

I looked down at the quarter of a tank and cursed. "I think there's a hotel a little further up. Let's see if we can shelter there for a little bit."

"And you're okay driving on this that far?"

"It's less than a quarter of a mile. Let's just get off this road as soon as possible."

"And we'll just stay there until the storm passes and we'll go home. I told Faith I wasn't going to stay the night."

"I'll get you home to your little girl, Ava. I promise."

I met her gaze, and she nodded tightly, before gripping my arm. "Just be safe. No heroics?"

"Those are my cousins. They're the heroes. I'm just going to get us safely there."

She nodded again, before I pulled back out onto the road, going so slow I was pretty sure snails could pass us.

Cars continued to move down the road as I turned off toward the motel with a vacancy sign. "I'm going to hop out and make sure that that vacancy sign is true; do you want to stay here in the warm car?"

She shook her head. "No. Let's save the gas just in case." She shivered. "And doesn't that sound ominous?"

We pulled on our coats though they weren't thick enough for this type of weather and made our way into the small lobby and to the registration desk. The place smelled of old smoke and mold, but I didn't care. It was warm, and there was a café attached to the lobby.

"Looks like you made it just in time. This storm is seeming to settle over us. It isn't going to stop for a few hours. We've got one more room, do you want it?" the older woman with dark curly hair and horned rim glasses said, and I looked towards Ava.

She looked over her shoulder as another car pulled into the parking lot and stepped closer.

"We'll take it."

"Okay, sign here. We'll get you in for the night. Anyone else, well they can stay at the diner, or here in the lobby, I guess. We'll keep everyone warm and safe."

The lady sounded like she was talking to herself at

this point, but I pulled out my wallet and gave the woman my card.

Ava glanced at me, and I shrugged. "I've got it. It's a work expense."

She raised a brow, but it was true. She was here because I had wanted her to be with me. Because I hadn't thought this through.

I couldn't want Ava like this. There were so many reasons we shouldn't be together. Namely, when we broke up, because we would, we would hurt Faith and each other. And all of us had been hurt enough as it was.

I was not going to shatter that little girl's heart, nor bruise Ava's any more than it already was.

And yet I invited her here as if I had any right to do so.

I was the damn problem here, and I knew it.

I needed to do better. And stop making such rash decisions when it came to Ava.

"Okay, there you go. The door faces the outside, but you're going to be able to see your car from the window. Get yourself something to eat from the café before it gets too busy and stay warm. If I am not here when you need to check out, if you want to get out early once the storm settles, my son will be here. We've got you."

The woman and her raspy voice did her best to soothe us, but knowing I'd have to spend a few hours, if not the entire night alone in a room with Ava? This was going to suck.

"Okay, let's go get our stuff," Ava said, then frowned. "Not that we have stuff. I don't even have a toothbrush."

"I've got one left," the lady said, and handed it over. "I'm sorry. You're going to have to share."

She gave us a knowing look, but I took the toothbrush and we headed back to my SUV.

"So, I'm trying not to panic, but I feel like I'm panicking."

"Don't worry, we can panic together. Come on. It shouldn't be that long. Hopefully we can check the local news and figure out what's going on."

"I need to get ahold of Faith. I don't want her to be worried about me."

"We'll get a message out. I think I saw a phone behind the desk, and I am sure they have one in the room. So if we don't get cell service, we can call my brothers from one of them, or something."

"I don't even know your phone number by heart. Oh my God, how did we get to a place where I don't have any numbers memorized?"

"You're just panicking. We can look in the contacts of your phone, babe. We can charge them too. You're fine. We're not completely in the Dark Ages."

Ava winced. "Please don't make fun of me."

"Oh, I'm going to make fun of you because it'll lighten the situation."

"Will it? Or will it make me feel like I'm losing my damn mind?"

"Why don't you go to the room, and I'll get us something to eat before they run out. Shouldn't be here more than a couple hours."

"I don't think you can promise that," she said softly.

"No, I can't. But I can hope for the best because I don't really know what else to do right now. I am sorry for getting you into this."

"I could have said no. It's not your fault. I just wanted to do something worthwhile to prove that I earned this job."

I frowned. "You earned this, Ava. You're damn good at what you do."

"We don't need to get into this right now."

"Maybe we should. Because you earned this job. Yeah, I gave it to you at first because you were a friend in need, but fuck that. We would've found something else for you to do if you sucked at it. We're Wilders: we're smart, loyal, but we make decisions that keep our businesses afloat."

"You're a good person, Wyatt."

I shook my head. "I'm not. Go on, get inside, and I'll go get us some food."

"Okay. This won't take long."

"Damn right it won't," I grumbled, before I made my way to the café and picked up a couple of burgers and fries and drinks. It wasn't much, but it would hold us for a few hours. I didn't even know if she was hungry, but I just needed to keep Ava safe.

We had been lucky on that road, and if I had been thinking, we wouldn't have been out there to begin with.

But I hadn't been thinking, and now I needed to deal with this.

I got back to the room and knocked on the door with my foot since I had piled all the food in my arms. I heard the chain rustling, and I was glad that she was taking safety precautions as she opened the door.

"I got ahold of Faith and your brother. Ridge and Aurora are going to take her for the night, thank God. Your family's amazing." She took a step back before reaching for a couple of the bags in my arms.

"How much food did you get?" she asked.

"Enough." My gaze centered on the one bed, and then back at Ava.

"We didn't really specify what room we wanted, and there was only the one. So, we'll deal with it. I can sleep in the tub."

"For fuck's sake, we can sleep in the same bed, Ava. Although, maybe we can't. We haven't been in a bed."

She grinned, as did I, and the heat between us began

to sizzle. And that was a mistake because we were not going to do that again. Not when I would just hurt her in the end. Since there wasn't a table or anything in the small room, we sat on the bed with a towel underneath our food, and I turned on the news.

"The storm should only last a few more hours."

"But then it'll be night, and the ice won't be able to melt. It might not be until early in the morning before we can leave. Not the best way to celebrate right before your mom gets here for Christmas."

"I got ahold of her too, and she's watching the storm path as well. They're getting hammered up there. Flights all over the country are being canceled. This sucks."

"It does suck that all the family gatherings happen during the worst parts of our weather."

"I guess it's a godsend to those who don't actually want to see their family."

"That is true," I said as I stuffed a french fry in my mouth. We were sitting side by side, and I could feel the heat of her as we ate our burgers and fries.

"These are actually delicious," she said, and I grunted an acknowledgment.

"Honestly, I wasn't expecting much, but the room is clean enough."

"You're right. And it smells like laundry soap. The

lady was nice, and the food is good. So I'm going to pretend that everything's okay and I'm not panicking."

"That sounds like a good idea," I said with a sigh, and we finished eating. We cleaned up, and then found ourselves standing in front of each other, awkward as fuck.

"You want to see if there's a movie on cable? Or whatever passes for cable?"

"Sure. I don't know what to sleep in. These slacks won't be too comfortable."

"I was just going to sleep in my boxers and my undershirt. Next time I guess we'll bring an overnight bag. You know, considering my cousin once had to stay somewhere overnight because of a tornado."

Her eyes widened. "Are you serious?"

"Dead serious. Everyone was okay, but after that, I should have been more prepared."

We got ready for the night, though it was still a little too early to go to bed, and shared that one toothbrush, then got into bed, me in my boxers and an undershirt, her in a long sleeve shirt she had had in her bag and panties.

I caught a flash of skin as she buried herself under the covers, and I remembered tasting those thighs, my hands on them as I craved more. I swallowed, then tilted my hips away so she wouldn't see my erection.

Of course, her gaze went right to it, and I cursed.

"Ignore him. He's just happy to see you."

Her lips twitched. "This is ridiculous."

"Very much so. Let's just get some sleep or something."

"Put a movie on?" she suggested.

We both nodded, ignoring whatever was going on between us, and put on a movie with subtitles that was black and white and grainy. The perfect thing to capture my attention.

We turned off the lights, buried under the covers, and did our best not to touch.

Except I could still feel the heat of her, and every time I shifted, she did too, so the rustling of blanket over her skin nearly sent me over the edge.

Her hand brushed mine and we both froze, before I let out a cursed breath and turned to the side, giving her my back, pretending to sleep.

When her relieved sigh filled the room, I knew I had done the right thing, and as I willed myself to sleep, I listened to the choppiness of her breaths and told myself that this was for the greater good.

Nothing good could come from Ava and me sleeping together again.

Thankfully, I drifted off to sleep, except I dreamed that Ava was hot and warm against me, her breasts filling my hands as I rocked my erection onto her backside. She hummed as I slid my hand between her legs, under her panties. Her folds were wet, soaking my hand as I fingered her slowly, using my middle finger to press deep inside her, my pointer finger rubbing her clit. She shivered, reaching around to grip my cock underneath my boxers. As she continued to stroke me, that little bead of moisture at the tip of my cock pressed against her back, leaving a wet spot. She was so tight around my finger, so I inserted another one, loving the way that she moaned. And when she came, she shivered, rocking back into me.

That's when my eyes opened and realized that it wasn't a dream. My fingers were between her legs, her hand at an awkward angle to try to get me off. Her shirt was off one shoulder, both of her breasts spilling out into my hand, and I had my mouth on her neck, sucking and biting so hard I knew there would be a bruise in the morning.

I froze as I realized what was happening, and then she did too, and that's when I realized we were both finally awake.

"Oh my God," she whispered.

"I can stop right now. I can move my fingers away; we could pretend it never happened. Or..." I let my voice trail off.

She was silent for so long, but she didn't let go of my cock.

"Or."

And then I was pressing her shoulders into the mattress, her panties to the side, and shoving into her from behind.

She let out a shocked gasp, and I pinned her to the bed, pounding into her with one thrust and then another.

"That's it. Take my cock. Let me fill you."

"Wyatt," she moaned into the bed.

"Yes, say my name. You're so tight this way. With your thighs pressed together and me sliding my dick deep inside you. Can you feel me? Do you want more? Can you take it?"

"Stop talking a big game and give it to me. All of it."

I leaned down and bit her throat again and she shivered, before pushing back and going to her hands and knees.

Elated, I gripped her hips and began to pummel into her, needing her.

I needed her so damn much it was hard to breathe, and I knew this was a mistake.

But in the moment of bliss I didn't care.

She met me thrust for thrust. When I slid my hands over her back and down her backside so I could play with that little hole, she shivered.

"Do you want me to fuck your ass? If I had lube, I would totally fuck your ass, take it and claim it as mine."

"Only if I can watch," she whispered.

"Damn straight. That's my girl."

I hadn't even realized I was saying the words until my finger was playing with her backside, using her own wetness as lube. I slid one finger inside her to the knuckle, and she tightened around me, letting out little mewing sounds. I continued to move, using my other hand on her clit to keep her going, and when she came again, I followed.

My balls tightened and my whole body shook. I filled her up and claimed her as mine, in every primal sense of the word. She was so fucking beautiful.

We lay together for a moment, and I knew this was a problem.

I was the problem.

I slid out of her and kissed her softly, cupping her face with one hand.

"Let me clean you up."

"Okay," she whispered.

We showered together in silence, a sense of foreboding sliding over us.

Because if this kept going, I would hurt her and Faith. And I couldn't do that. We each got dressed, both of us putting on our pants this time, and sat on the bed facing each other.

"We need to stop doing that," she said quietly, and I nodded.

"It can't happen again," I said, but this time my voice was far firmer than it had been.

She met my gaze and frowned. "I know why I can't have this happen again. What about you?"

"I think it's the same reason," I said softly.

"Faith," we said at the same time.

"When this goes south, I'm going to hurt that little girl. I won't mean to, but I will. And Aaron already did a number on her."

"You're right. He screwed up so much. And while that wasn't your fault, I can't bring someone into her life in that way again. So, we can just remain friends. I see the way you two are around each other. She likes you. And she needs men in her life. But I can't bring you in like that."

I gave her a small smile, one that ached. "You're right. There's another thing too."

She frowned. "What?"

"Did you ever wonder why Isabelle and I never had kids?" I asked, wondering why I was even saying these things.

"No. That's not something you ask unless they bring it up. And Isabelle, well, we weren't friends."

I cringed at that. "That should have been the first sign."

"You and I never got along."

"Well, I have a feeling it had more to do with this," I

said, pointing between us, "than anything else. But I digress." I took a deep breath, knowing I needed to just say it. "I made a promise when I was eighteen that I would do my best never to have children."

Her eyes widened. "What? But you're great with kids."

"I'm great with other people's kids. But my girlfriend in high school, well, we weren't as careful as we should have been. Since you and I have yet to be careful." Which was so unlike me and against what I'd told myself so many years ago. Something I needed to be so damn careful with. Because I'd hurt us both in the end.

She cringed. "Oh, Wyatt."

I looked off into the distance for a moment before turning back to her. "It was a late term miscarriage. We didn't realize what was happening until it was happening, and then the baby was gone, and I hadn't even realized I had wanted that baby. I was barely a man, ready to head into college and try to figure out my life, and I had gotten my girlfriend pregnant. I was going to step up, my dad made sure of that. My parents hadn't been disappointed in me, but they had been worried. And then the baby died, and my girlfriend, though she was an amazing person, didn't love me. And I didn't love her the way I needed to either. But that feeling? That feeling of wondering how I was going to be as a father? I lost that. I lost that in an instant and I told myself I would never do that again. And I know it's not logical, but that's what I've been telling myself since I was eighteen. And yet, seeing you with Faith? Being with her when I'm just hanging out with the two of you, or seeing her running around the compound? That little girl is everything. And, well, it's not that I don't want to feel that pain again, because that would be a selfish thing."

"It wouldn't, Wyatt, it wouldn't."

I reached forward and wiped her tears away from her face. She was crying for me. For a child that hadn't even had a chance to take its first breath. And that was the Ava that I started to fall for. The Ava that I needed to keep away from.

"Your kid? She's fucking amazing. And if you and I putter out, or if we break each other's hearts, I'm going to break her. And I promised myself I would never let another child into my life that could get hurt. Not in that way. So I'm going to be the best fucking uncle to all of my nieces and nephews and cousins. And I'm going to be a good friend to Faith. But you and me? We would hurt her. I don't want to become Aaron."

"Damn it," Ava said, and for an instant I was afraid I had said the wrong thing. Instead, she leaned forward and cupped my face. "That makes you stronger than you'll ever know. You will always be her friend." She let out a shaky and watery breath. "And I trust you for that." She leaned back and wiped her face. "So we won't fall in love, Wyatt. We'll be strong. And will make sure that we remain friends. For Faith. And maybe for us. But you're right. Falling into bed would hurt us in the end. And hurt Faith. So we won't. And we're adults. We can do this."

"So, just friends?"

"Just friends," she whispered. "And, Wyatt? Thank you for trusting me with that secret."

My lungs hurt as I nodded. "I don't think about that often. Sometimes it just hits me."

"I understand. And if you ever want to talk, I'm here. Because we're friends, Wyatt."

There was something in her tone, something I couldn't read, and didn't want to dive deeper into. I just nodded and checked the weather. And when she fell asleep, fully dressed, I tucked her in and watched her sleep.

And told myself this was for the best.

It had to be.

CHAPTER THIRTEEN

AVA

By the time we made it home early the next morning, I was a wreck, and needed to shower for more reasons than one.

Faith had had the time of her life apparently, with Aurora and Ridge making a blanket and pillow fort in the living room for her. The ice and snow hadn't been as bad closer to the Wilders as it had been where we were, which just goes to show that the weather gods hated me.

However, now I was back in my cabin, working on setting up the place for the Christmas holidays.

The fact that I didn't have a real tree or any ornaments made my heart ache for Faith, but we were making do.

Everything had happened so quickly, and it still

didn't feel like this place was ours. Probably because it wasn't. It was just the two of us in this little borrowed cabin as we figured out exactly how we were going to make our way through the season.

"Mom, what do you think of this?" Faith asked from the doorway, and I looked up from my computer where I had been working on something for Wyatt and the bar. Faith held a long paper chain that had far more days than we had until Christmas.

"Is that for New Year's?" I asked with a laugh.

"Of course. Everybody else does paper chains for Christmas, but I wanted New Year's because I am not a baby anymore."

She said it so primly that I had to force myself not to smile, but instead nod sagely.

"Understandable. The new year is something to celebrate. It wipes the slate clean and you can look forward to something new."

Faith moved forward shyly as she clambered up onto the bed, leaving the paper art project at the edge.

"Do you think this new school will like me?"

My heart did that twisting thing again. I pulled her close, wrapping my arm around her.

"I think they will. What's not to love or like?"

"But Dad doesn't love me."

I swallowed hard, anger mixing with pure agony.

If I could go back in time and never be with Aaron, I would. And yet I wouldn't have my daughter.

It was an odd dichotomy of hatred for the man who had given me my daughter, and love for the daughter who had given me everything else.

All I wanted to do was find a way to make it up to her, to show her that she was beautiful and loving and amazing and deserving of love.

And yet, Aaron's lack of attention and cruelty kept undermining that.

"I love you so much, my darling."

Faith nuzzled into me, wrapping one arm around my waist. The warm wetness of tears covered my shoulder, and I cursed the day I thought I had fallen in love with Aaron.

"I love you, too. I just wish Daddy did."

I didn't have words for this. Though we had talked about it before, she hadn't been so blatant. The right words felt like they would never come. Because this was my daughter, my precious daughter. And there wasn't anything I could say to make this better. So perhaps the holidays, and even watching the way that the Wilders cared for their kids, and Faith, had brought this out. But I knew I would need to try to make it better. Even if I couldn't.

"I don't know why your dad acts the way he does. I don't have any excuses for him. And you are old enough to know that he hurt me, but that doesn't mean he's allowed to hurt you."

"He's not allowed to hurt you either."

I nodded against the top of her head, running my hand down her back.

"You're right. He doesn't have the right to do any of that. I don't have answers or reasons. I just hope one day he realizes that he missed out on so much. He's missing out on knowing the best girl I know. You are a thrill to be around, and a person I love knowing. I am better because you are in my life. I am blessed because I have you. I don't know what he's going to do once he realizes what he lost out on."

"Why doesn't he love me?"

Ice slid through my heart, cold and fiery at the same time. I squeezed my daughter tightly, not knowing what to say. The idea that I was at a loss for words to make my child feel loved and wanted made me feel like the worst mother ever.

"I don't know what's going on in your father's head. I'm not going to lie to you and pretend. But one day he's going to open his eyes and realize that he made a mistake. I don't have the words to make this better. I'm not going to lie. I would though if I thought it would make you feel better. I would lie and say that he was trying hard, but I don't want to lie to you."

"I like that you don't lie. And I like Wyatt. Wyatt

and Ridge and Brooks and Eli and all the others are so nice to me. It's not like having a dad, but that's okay because I don't need one. Not really."

"Oh, baby."

"I don't. I have you, and I have Rory, and I have all the Wilders. They're the best. So I know I'm not alone. I just...I don't know if I like Daddy right now."

She sniffed, and I did too, holding my baby even tighter.

"You don't have to like him right now. I am not going to tell you that you have to. You don't have to like anyone once you try your best to. You just need to be yourself and love yourself. Okay? There is nothing lacking in you. Whatever your dad is feeling is not on you. You are loved. You are wonderful. You are kind, you are gracious. You are the light of my life, and some-times my reason for waking up in the mornings. I love watching you grow and breathe and just be.

"So just know that you are loved. And one day your daddy's going to wake up and realize what he missed."

"Do I have to forgive him?"

My hand squeezed her shoulder, because I had answers that I wanted to say, but knew it would be better if I didn't.

"I think that's up to you and what you're feeling and what happens. I do know that hating someone and feeling that hurt all the time is not good for you. So you do what works to make you happy. I love you so much. Please know that."

"I do. I never doubt that you do. I'm going to go work on more paper chains. I promised Wyatt I would make him one."

That little squeeze on my heart happened again.

Wyatt and I were trying to do our best to keep away from each other in that way so Faith wouldn't get hurt. She was already feeling the lack because of Aaron. Wyatt and I would do whatever we could to make sure it wasn't going to happen to Faith because of him too. I kissed the top of her head and she scrambled away, skipping as if she hadn't just laid her heart bare to me. But that was my resilient daughter.

Aaron had tried to shatter that, even if unintentionally. So keeping Wyatt away from my heart so we could protect Faith's was the smart idea.

Even though I was such a fucking liar to myself. I had already gone and fallen for him. I had made yet another mistake. One I would have to rectify by keeping Faith at the front of my mind.

Wyatt had been hurt as well, and my heart ached for him. So I wasn't going to be the one who broke both.

I would just break myself. But that was my own choice.

I rubbed my temples and told myself to get in the

game. I had a job that I was thriving at and that I enjoyed. I had friends who I was learning I could rely on, which was a shocking development. And my little girl was happy. Yes, her heart was bruised, but she was also smiling and excited for the holidays. I even had enough money to actually buy a few presents, though nothing too extravagant. We were still learning our way with that.

This wasn't going to be the Christmas that we wanted, or like any that we'd had before. But we were together, and that was going to have to be enough.

My phone buzzed and I answered it quickly after seeing my mother's name on the readout. She was supposed to be on a plane soon, and I was going to pick her up at the San Antonio International Airport.

"Mom? What's wrong?"

"Baby. I'm so sorry, but they canceled our flight. There's a blizzard in Detroit."

My eyes began to sting, and I blinked away whatever silly tears were going to come. Because I wasn't going to cry. No. This was fine. Everything was fine. I was just telling myself how many blessings I had. There was no reason to cry because my mommy wasn't going to be here for Christmas.

"Oh."

"I'm so sorry. We're just now leaving the airport, we tried everything. And we didn't want to worry you until we had answers, because I know you're doing so much. Pierre and I are devastated."

I swallowed hard, but my mother couldn't see me, and I just looked at the phone, wondering what I was supposed to do.

Faith was going to be devastated. I was devastated.

"Baby? I'm sorry. We're going to make it out there as soon as they reschedule our flights. I know it won't be Christmas Day, and we'll probably lose our reservation with the Wilders, but that's fine. We're coming to see you. I need to hug my grandbaby. Ava? Darling? Are you there?"

"Mom," I whispered, my voice breaking. I hadn't even realized it was all pent up until the tears were falling and it felt like someone was ripping my heart from me. I tried to be quiet so Faith wouldn't hear me, and thankfully she had her show on. I didn't want Faith to see me like this.

"Pull over, pull over, honey. Ava, what's wrong? I know you're disappointed. So am I, but this isn't just about that, is it? What are these tears from, baby?"

"I just really needed you here. It's been a really, really long year."

And then I did the thing I should have done earlier. I told her everything. About Aaron. About the cheating and the divorce and the small apartment. About having the job that I hated and feeling unsafe. About moving to the Wilders because I had nowhere else to go. I told her about Faith's college fund and losing everything else, and when I was done, I wiped the snot from under my nose, the tears from my face, and knew I had made a mistake in not telling my mother sooner. I just wanted my mommy to hold me, just like I had held Faith.

But nothing seemed to be going right. I was in love with a man that couldn't love me back, and once again I was making the same mistakes.

"Ava, darling. Why didn't you tell me any of this?"

"I'm sorry, Mom."

"No, I'm not going to make this about me. I know you probably kept everything to yourself because you wanted to be strong and handle it and not burden me, but we're going to have a talk about this when we're in person and I can hold you. But for right now take a deep breath, wash your face, and know that you are loved. And know that if it wasn't for this blizzard, your stepfather and I would be flying out to go kick that man's ass. What the hell was Aaron thinking? And your lawyer couldn't do anything?"

"No. He had a better one."

"Well, fuck him. And your lawyer. Just fuck all of them."

I let out a laugh, tears still streaming down my cheeks. "Mother!"

"What? I'm allowed to say curse words."

On the other end of the line, I heard my stepfather also cursing but laughing at the same time. For some reason that thought warmed me. I didn't know my stepfather well, mostly because I didn't get to see him often, but he had always been kind and a wonderful grandfather to Faith. I didn't know why I kept forgetting that I had more in my life than I thought possible.

I needed to cling to that.

"As soon as we're able, we're getting on a plane and we're coming to visit. You know what, fuck it, I'm just going to walk there. I'm sure we can drive there faster at this point, who cares about a blizzard?"

"Mom, just get here when you can safely. I'll explain it to Faith. And we'll celebrate when you're here. I just really wanted to tell you everything. I should have done that to begin with."

"Yes, you should have. And I love you so freaking much, my darling."

"I love you too."

"Good. You remember that. Now, we need to get back on the road because the snow is coming down a little bit more, and then I'll call you back and we're going to have a lovely video chat to talk about the holidays. And when it's time, we can go murder Aaron and put him in the backyard. Nobody's going to miss him."

"Mom!"

"Okay, maybe not murder. Maybe a little maiming. No one ever got mad about maiming."

"I love you so much."

"I love you too. I'm sorry we're not going to be there. And that the two of you are going to be alone for Christmas."

I cleared my throat. "I don't think we can be alone. I'm surrounded by Wilders."

My mom laughed, and I was grateful for that.

"By a certain Wilder?" she hedged.

And I shook my head even though she couldn't see me.

"No. I don't have a Wilder. They're all loving to Faith."

"Okay. We're going to call back soon. I love you. I'm so sorry for everything."

"I'm sorry too. But we'll see you soon. I promise. Even if I must fly up there."

"We have miles. We'll get you up here as long as we don't interfere with Faith's new school. Oh my, so many changes."

"Tell me about it."

I finally let her go and did as my mother told me, and I washed my face, letting the ice-cold water help ease the redness and puffiness.

I pulled my hair back in a ponytail and then went

out to meet Faith. This wasn't going to be the holiday that we wanted, but we would find a way.

"Hey, Mom. I'm finished with Wyatt's paper present."

"It looks lovely," I said, looking at the rainbow-colored paper chain she had made.

"I didn't know what color to do so I did all of them."

"That works."

"What's wrong?" she asked, and I held out my arms. Faith ran into me and I held her close.

"Your grandma and Pierre are stuck in Canada for a few more days. There's a huge storm over the Midwest and it's ruining flights. I'm so sorry, baby."

Faith let out a huge sigh, her shoulders dropping. "That sucks. But we'll still get to see her later, right?"

I nodded. "Yes, you're taking this much better than me."

"Because I have my mommy. You just want yours."

How this little girl, who sometimes couldn't remember how to knock before she walked into my bedroom, could be so insightful shouldn't surprise me, but it did.

"You are so wise for your years, my darling."

"Of course I am. I have you as a mommy."

"I love you, you dork."

I kissed the top of her head when the doorbell rang.

I frowned, wondering who it could be. Faith skipped over to the door, and I rolled my eyes, following her.

When she looked through the window she began to clap, and I had a feeling I knew exactly who it was.

"Wyatt!" Faith said as she opened the door wide. "I have your present."

"That's the best news ever. Hello, girls," he said, and I ignored the way my heart flipped.

We were just friends. Because it was safer.

"Oh. I didn't know you were coming."

"I just realized that you guys might be missing something for the holidays, so I thought I'd bring it by." And then he pulled out a three-foot-tall Christmas tree from beside him.

"It's fake, because all our family has allergies, but it is pre-lit. So that should help. All you need to do is add ornaments."

"A Christmas tree!" Faith said. "It's beautiful. I love it." She threw her arms around Wyatt, who caught her and picked her up.

He was so damn strong that he made my eight-year-old look like a toddler.

"You didn't have to do that."

"Of course we did. It's your first Christmas in the cabin. I should have thought about it earlier, but I've had other things on my mind." He met my gaze for an instant and then we each looked away, that heat annoying me.

"I wish we had ornaments," Faith said sadly, resting her head on his shoulder.

He frowned. "Oh. Since you brought everything over from your place, I thought you might have some. It's okay, I have extras. I can bring them over."

It felt like another punch to the gut, but that was what today was for apparently.

"It's okay. The ornaments are, well, they didn't make this trip," I said, trying to be as casual as possible. Faith didn't seem to notice as she scrambled down Wyatt's large body and made her way to her craft corner where she had her presents.

He leaned forward, his voice low. "They at Aaron's?"

"If he didn't throw them away. It was one of the boxes he stole before I had a chance to go through them. And I couldn't fight for everything. There were only so many battles, you know?"

He cursed under his breath, and I raised a brow.

"You're not supposed to say that word," Faith said with a laugh as she came back with the paper chain in one hand and a drawing in the other.

"Sorry, you're with us Wilders, we curse a lot. I'll do better."

"It's okay. Mommy curses too."

I rolled my eyes. "Thanks for that."

"I try," Faith said as she fluttered her eyelashes.

Wyatt took both art projects from Faith and bent down so he was at her eye level.

"You made these?"

"Yep. Just for you."

He smiled so sweetly at my daughter and that damn tug ached again. The tug I needed to forget.

"I love it, Faith. Thank you."

I looked at him. "Why don't we set up the paper chains and things on the tree, and you can stay for dinner? I was just making some pasta."

"You sure?" he asked, his voice low.

"Please, Wyatt? Please stay? Mom makes great pasta."

He met my gaze, then Faith's, and smiled. "Yeah, I will."

When he closed the door behind him, leaving him and the tree in the small cabin with us, I knew absolutely nothing.

This treading upon a friendship path wasn't going to be easy, but for Faith? I would do anything.

Even if it hurt more than I could breathe.

CHAPTER FOURTEEN
WYATT

"Why the hell am I doing this?" I grumbled to myself as I used my turn signal and passed the slow-moving car in front of me. It didn't matter what time of day it was, as soon as you were in South Texas, everybody had to go lower than the speed limit. I did not understand it. It was a highway with a speed limit of seventy miles per hour, and the guy in front of me? Going fifty-five. That probably wasn't helping my stress and anxiety levels when it came to what I needed to do next.

Mainly, try not to make a damn fool of myself.

Ava hadn't asked this of me. Honestly, I was surprised she had even mentioned what Aaron had done. But I saw the look on her face when she mentioned those ornaments. And noticed that Faith hadn't even blinked twice at the idea that she wasn't going to have a full Christmas tree this year. Oh, Ava had decorated the place nicely, with garland and other things she had gotten at the dollar store down the road. But she hadn't bought a Christmas tree, because of allergies, and the fact that she probably didn't know where she was going to be next Christmas. This whole thing was supposed to have been temporary while she got back on her feet and got Faith settled in her new school. Christmas trees weren't something at the top of the list. But I knew for a fact that little girl was going to have all the Christmas presents she could ever want, because she was a damn good kid, and Ava was an even better mother.

Plus, we Wilders were going to make sure that Faith was not lost amongst the busyness of a holiday season.

Ava was doing everything she could for her kid, but that rat bastard had done everything to make it that much harder for her.

I couldn't believe I'd ever been friends with that man. We had hung out for years, taken group vacations together. When my brothers weren't in my life as much as I had wanted, I'd had Aaron.

At least, that's what I'd thought.

It made me feel as if I had made one bad decision after another when it came to my life. How could I ever trust my judgment again, or any decision I had made or would make. After all, I had thought Aaron was my best friend, and Isabelle was the one woman I would ever love.

I took the exit off the highway and made my way towards Aaron's place. I was such a damn idiot. This was going to lead to nowhere. There was a high probability that Aaron didn't even have the damn ornaments. But once I had really thought about it, I realized that Ava had spoken about those ornaments before. Long ago when Faith had been just a toddler and I'd held her on my hip as she had laughed and giggled and we had put a sparkly little ball on the tree, Ava had talked about those ornaments.

"This one's from my great-great-grandmother," Ava had said. "And this one? From her daughter. We've had these in our family for generations. Some have broken, but the remaining ones just make me happy." She had smiled softly up at Aaron, who had such a loving expression on his face, that I would never have known that Aaron would turn out to be a snake in the grass.

But Aaron had to have known what those ornaments meant to her. That Ava would've wanted them for herself and Faith.

And so here I was, probably about to make a fool of myself.

There was no way that me being here was smart. This was just asking for issues. I hadn't even seen

Aaron since he'd stopped by with Isabelle that night. This was a mistake.

But I couldn't get Ava's expression out of my head. I wanted to make sure that pain she felt never happened again. Not that it was my right to do something about it, but as her friend, even with how murky that situation was with us, I wanted to do better by her.

And if I kept rationalizing this to myself, it would all make sense.

Shaking my head at myself, I turned right at the light and headed into Aaron's neighborhood. It was a different place than the one that he had lived with Ava. He had gotten the house and taken everything, from what I could tell, then moved into a new house with Isabelle, but in the same neighborhood. I was so angry that Ava had lost so much in the divorce, but I had watched so many people get screwed out of what they deserved because not everybody were good people.

We'd known that for a long time now.

It was just the evidence of that being thrown in our face wasn't something I liked to think about.

But here I was, putting myself into a situation that did not have anything to do with me. But then again, maybe it had everything to do with me.

Because if Aaron wasn't going to stand up for Faith, then I would.

Because that little girl needed protectors.

And Ava? Well, she did too, not that I let myself think like that. Because she wouldn't want that. And it was better if we didn't think about each other like that.

I knew this was a mistake, but I had to do what was right. Even if it didn't make any sense. So I pulled in front of Aaron's house, one he shared with Isabelle, and turned off the engine. I was just going to go in and ask. Maybe Aaron didn't have them, maybe he would keep them just for spite. But no matter what, I needed to try.

I reminded myself this was for Faith.

But in reality, it was for Ava too.

I got out of the car and made my way up the path to the front door. The two of them had bought a nice little one-story ranch house, what they used to call a "starter home" for a couple. Interesting, considering that Aaron had taken all of his and Ava's money. He should have been able to afford a bigger house. Or maybe they had a beach house and a Jet Ski and a boat and all that shit. I didn't know, and it wasn't my place to judge them. After all, I lived in a cabin on my family's property because I had invested in it. Who was I to judge?

Except that this was Aaron and Isabelle so of course I was going to fucking judge them.

The door opened before I could even knock, and Isabelle stood there. Her hair flowed down her shoulders, her eyes smoky. She had done that cat eye thing with her eyeliner, which she had spent months learning to get right and would yell at me if I didn't compliment them right away. I'd always thought she had beautiful eyes with or without makeup, and if she wanted to spend time figuring out that look, I was all for it. But sometimes I didn't pay attention enough. At least according to her.

Yes, there were probably mistakes made on both sides in our marriage, but she had been the one who cheated. She had been the one to leave.

I wasn't sure what else I was supposed to do about that.

I didn't like that it was Isabelle that I was seeing first right now.

I would've much rather it been anyone else. No, that was a lie, because the only other person it could have been was Aaron. And while I needed to talk to him, I didn't want to deal with the asshole.

"This is a surprise. Are you my Christmas present?"

She had a wine glass in her hand, which I was just now realizing, and I had a feeling it was probably not her first glass. From the way that those smoky eyes were a little bit glassy, and she had slurred her greeting, I wondered how much wine she'd had.

I was in the business of making booze. My family made wine. Though it would've been ironic if she was drinking Wilder wine so I wasn't going to ask. But it was still early in the day and she was probably already smashed.

What the hell had happened to her?

I used to ask what happened to us, but that didn't matter anymore.

Because I was better off without her.

Huh. That was nice to think. I was better off without her.

And yet the one person I wanted I couldn't have because it would risk too much. But a small part of me told me I was making a mistake with that too.

But this wasn't the time to think about that.

"Isabelle, I'm here to see Aaron."

"Oh. How sad." She stuck her lower lip out and pouted.

"Is he here?"

"He's out back. We're having a barbecue before we go on vacation for Christmas. No need to stay home, you know. Like you always made me do."

That was a lie. The four of us had gone on a Christmas cruise one year, while Faith had stayed with her grandma. It had been a shitty cruise filled with seasickness and fighting, but there had been fun.

And if it hadn't been for the deal we had gotten, we wouldn't have gone at all.

I didn't recognize the woman standing in front of me. How had I loved her?

Or maybe it was that age-old thing where people change, and you didn't know who you'd become until you looked in the mirror and realized you weren't the person that fit with that other one anymore.

Had Isabelle realized that before she cheated? Or had she just gone and done it because she'd wanted to? Sadly that seemed more likely.

"I'm just here to see Aaron," I repeated.

"He'll be out in a bit. Let's talk."

I met Isabelle's eyes and felt nothing.

No dread, no anger. Certainly not love. I hadn't loved her for longer than I cared to admit. I suppose that was on me for sticking with it for as long as I had. Maybe if I had been the one to walk away, it wouldn't have been this messy. Then again, I had trusted her, just like I thought she had loved me.

But I had been wrong.

"I keep texting you. Just like old times."

"And I keep ignoring you." I shook my head. "What's this about, Isabelle? You barely wanted to talk to me when we were married. Now that you're getting married to the supposed love of your life, you want to text me? It doesn't make any sense."

"You always held yourself back from me. I know why. And I respected that." I froze, not wanting to hear her say why. Of course, Isabelle knew about the baby.

She had known everything about me. I had loved her and bared my soul to her. What had I expected?

"Don't go there."

"Why? We were everything to each other."

"And you threw that away. Don't come back as if you care."

"But I do. I miss you."

What the hell was she on about? I had no idea what this woman wanted, but I had a feeling whatever it was would blow up in both of our faces if she didn't stop soon.

"Isabelle? Stop. Whatever you have going on doesn't look good on you."

"I used to look good on you." She stepped closer, putting her hand on my chest. I stepped back, even when she went on her tiptoes to try to kiss me.

"What the flying fuck?" I asked, staggering back. "Are you serious?"

"We were good together."

"And you're drunk."

The smell of booze—not just wine—wafting off her breath just then could have killed a horse.

"Isabelle, go get some water or something. Maybe some coffee. But don't fucking touch me again."

"I miss you."

"Go away. I shouldn't have fucking come."

"But you did. Don't you think it's fate?"

Then she stiffened, her whole body straightening, as if she just remembered someone else was in the house. Aaron came forward, a scowl on his face and a beer in his hand.

"What the fuck are you doing here?"

"Good to see you too. I'm here for Ava's things."

"Why the hell do you care about that bitch?"

I ignored Isabelle as she stared between us, confusion on her face.

"I would tell you to watch the way that you are talking about the mother of your child, but we both know you have never cared about that."

"I'm not sure why it's your problem. Or why you think it is."

"How about this, you let me get what I need and I won't come back. That is, unless you make me come back. I'm just here to get a few things for the girls for Christmas."

"The girls. Oh." He threw his head back and laughed. "So, you're fucking my ex. That's nice." He wrapped his arm around Isabelle and pulled her to his side. "Tit for tat. Or is it tit for tit?"

"Oh stop," Isabelle teased, running her nails down his chest. "We both know he wouldn't be with someone as frigid as Ava. I was surprised you were."

"I came to learn the errors of my ways." He kissed

the top of her head. "But no. You aren't coming in here. Everything in this house is mine."

"Because you stole it from her. I'm not here to take your fucking TV or anything important to you. All I want is stuff that's from Ava's family. Come on. Do it for Faith."

"Don't you dare say my daughter's name."

"Why not? You aren't."

I should have known the punch was coming, as he shoved Isabelle to the side and swung his fist toward my face. However, I hadn't been expecting it because Isabelle had been standing between us before everything changed. She fell to the ground, and the first hit landed on my chin. Stars shot behind my eyes and I cursed, staggering back. But when the second fist came, I was far more ready and grabbed his wrist and twisted. Aaron let out a screech as he tried to pull away.

"First shot's free. I don't know what's up with you, but I'm done. Now, get your fiancée up off the ground since you just pushed her down and we'll call this even. Otherwise I'll kick your ass."

"Fucking cunt." He tried to kick me in the knee, and I sighed, moving back and slamming my fist into Aaron's cheekbone.

My former best friend grunted and stumbled back as Isabelle clambered up, pulling him to her.

"Stop. The neighbors are going to see. Just give him

what he wants. It's not important. We don't want anything from that bitch anyway."

"He's fucking that cunt and we're supposed to just let him have what he wants?"

She glared at me as if she hadn't just tried to kiss me before all this happened and went to her tiptoes to stick her tongue down Aaron's throat.

I barely resisted the urge to throw up everything I had eaten that day.

"It's just us. Come on, we have vacation coming up. And so much more. We don't need him."

Something flashed across Aaron's eyes that I didn't understand. But then again, I didn't understand Aaron at all. All I knew was that I needed to get in there and get this damn box.

And ice my chin, because dear God it hurt like a motherfucker.

"Fine. What does she want?"

"First up, her family's ornaments. Then anything else nearby. Be kind for this Christmas holiday and just let her have her shit."

"Those damn ornaments. They are ugly as hell, and I was supposed to like them? No, we like new here." He squeezed Isabelle's ass, and she grinned.

"Just like we like you, baby."

She winked at me, and I had to wonder what kind of game she was playing.

"They're in the shed out back. Take whatever's labeled in her fucking handwriting. I don't care. I'm done."

"Why don't you sign something agreeing to that, just in case," I said, pulling out my phone. "So that way I have it on record."

"I'm not going to sue you."

I raised a brow, and he used the app that I hoped would be enough in court if needed. Not that I thought that Aaron would go through the process of suing me for taking a box. But he had already hit me once, who knew what he would do.

I made my way to the shed and looked at the piles of boxes that were in a haphazard stack. Some were damaged or waterlogged, and it hurt my heart because one of those had Faith's name on it.

Inside was just dirt and what looked to be a mouse habitat, so I knew that wasn't going to come with me. From what I could tell it was just old clothes, not memory boxes or anything. I also knew that Ava had been able to salvage some of it already, so Faith's baby book and all her records and things were safe. But as I looked in another box and saw a baby onesie that once must have fit Faith, my heart clenched.

Aaron had taken this because he could. Just to hurt Ava.

If I could hit the other man again, I would. Instead, I

pulled out everything that I could and stuffed it in the back of my SUV, including the box clearly labeled "ornaments." There were two more Christmas boxes, as well as a few things with Ava's name on it. All in all, I had ten boxes, and Aaron didn't even bother to check what I took. But he had signed it over, so I counted that as a win. I took a picture of everything that I could, and then closed the back before heading home.

I didn't bother to say goodbye. That ship had sailed long ago. And there was nothing left for us.

My jaw and fist ached the whole way home. I didn't even know why I had done it. But at least hopefully something good would come out of it. But I knew that this hadn't been my place.

What the hell was Ava going to think?

It was far too late for that, considering I had ten of her boxes. Before I knew it, I had made it past Wilder security and pulled up in front of her cabin. Feeling awkward, I turned off the engine and rubbed my temples. I wanted a beer, some ice for my chin, and to be alone.

Only, as I saw the smoke come from the chimney and realized they had a small fire going, and the twinkle lights on that I had helped put up in the windows, I realized maybe I didn't need to be alone.

When Ava opened the door and frowned at me, I finally got out of the car.

"I saw you sitting out here when the camera went off. Everything okay?"

She moved forward, her eyes widening. "Oh my God, Wyatt. Your chin."

"Wyatt?" Faith asked. The little girl came outside, but Ava held her back.

"Can you go inside and go get that blue ice pack? Wyatt will need it."

"Are you okay? Do you want me to kiss it and make it better?"

I smiled softly, my heart aching just a bit. "I'm okay, Faith. But that ice does sound good."

"I'll get it for you right now. And a sticker. Because stickers help everything."

She ran back and Ava stepped closer, facing me, putting her hand on my unbruised cheek. "What did you do?" she asked, the knowing in her gaze worrying me.

"I didn't throw the first punch."

"Aaron? Wyatt, what were you thinking?"

"I was thinking that I wanted to make sure that little girl got the Christmas she deserved."

"He doesn't need to be here. He doesn't want to be."

I shook my head before I pulled back and took her by her hand. I tugged her to the back of the car and pulled open the trunk.

"I didn't want him here. I wanted what was yours."

A shocked sigh sounded beside me, as I kept my hand on hers.

"How did you...? What...? How did this happen?"

"I asked. And well, he said yes. But don't worry. I made sure I got a paper trail of his agreement. He's not going to come after you for it."

Ava moved forward and looked at the smallest box on top. When she opened it, her eyes filled with tears.

"Don't cry. I didn't want you to cry."

"No. It's my grandma's. And this box has Faith's baby clothes. And this other box has some of my business work attire that I had wanted. It's just little things. Things we could have lived without, and had, but you got them for us."

She turned to me and pressed her lips against mine. I wrapped my arm around her waist and tugged her close, meeting the kiss.

"Will you come in for cocoa?" she asked, her voice soft. "As a thank you."

I looked past her as Faith ran towards us, icepack in hand, but I didn't let her go.

I knew this was a problem because I didn't want to feel this. This need and desire to be here with them. But I was already playing a losing game when it came to not wanting to be with Faith and Ava.

But maybe the mistake I had made was when I was

eighteen and had made that promise. That was something I would have to think about. But, right now, a little girl was handing me ice and I needed to keep smiling as she cheered and clapped her hands and looked at the boxes that had once been hers.

I would deal with what I wanted later, but now I would have that cocoa.

So I nodded and helped move the boxes, and pretended I knew what I wanted.

Even though, deep down, I was afraid I already did.

CHAPTER FIFTEEN
WYATT

"And this one is my favvvvooorite," Faith said with a laugh, drawing out the last word.

I leaned forward and smiled. "It looks great."

"This one is the one I made with Mom one Christmas. I don't remember which one it was. Do you?" Faith asked as she looked over her shoulder at Ava.

Ava stood in the doorway holding a cup of hot cocoa with a dazed expression on her face. Honestly, I didn't blame her. I felt a little dazed too.

I was helping finish trimming a Christmas tree for two people I knew I should walk away from. It would be easier for all involved if I did. But I wasn't going to. Instead I was part of this moment.

"That was from kindergarten," Ava finally answered,

pausing to set her mug next to mine. When she sat down cross-legged on the other side of Faith, I stood up.

She gave me a frown, but I just shook my head and went to look in another box. "Do you guys have a star? Or are you guys an angel or a bow family? These are important questions."

"We have a star, right, Mom?" Faith asked, and Ava nodded before she frowned.

"We should. I think it's in one of these boxes." Ava went to stand up, looking a little lost, but I held out my hand.

"Don't worry, I think I found it. We've got it, Ava. Don't worry." I repeated.

Once again, she gave me a look I couldn't read. Gratitude? Or maybe I had overstepped.

It felt as if I had overstepped. But the look she and Faith had gotten on their faces when we brought in all the boxes from my trunk meant that I would ignore any feeling of overstepping for a little while.

I dug around in the box and gestured for Faith to come over and stepped back when she let out a cheer.

"See? We do have a star. Thank you, Wyatt." With one hand still holding the pointed star, she wrapped her arms around my waist and hugged me tight. My throat tightened for a moment before I cleared it and looked over at Ava. Her eyes were shining with tears, and I sucked in a breath, telling myself that I needed to slow down, to breathe.

"Okay. So, who usually puts the star up?"

"We do, together."

"Let me get a chair or a stool," Ava said, and I shook my head.

"I can lift Faith. You want to help lift me?" I asked, giving her a wink.

She rolled her eyes, and then came forward, leaning against me for a moment before reaching out to help Faith.

I lifted Faith up quickly, and she set the star on the top of the tree like an expert, and then she was on the ground, and the three of us were hugging. And then Faith was moving to look at the next box, and Ava was going to help her, and I went to chug the rest of my cocoa, wishing there was some bourbon or something in it. Anything to cut through whatever I was feeling.

Faith stayed up for a little longer while we finished trimming the tree, and then somehow I was reading a Christmas book to her, telling her all about Scrooge and Christmas past and present. She giggled when I did the voices. Ava joined in, adding more voices of her own. When Faith began to add in voices that made us all laugh, I tapped her shoulder and raised a brow.

"You know, if we keep laughing like this, you're never going to bed."

She gave a jaw-cracking yawn right in my face and I burst out laughing. Ava just shook her head beside us. And then before Tiny Tim could tell us about the end of the book, Faith was passed out, blanket up to her chin, little snuffling noises escaping her nose.

She was seriously the cutest fucking thing.

We tiptoed out of Faith's room and turned off the lights, the nightlight in the corner glowing faintly. She had a tiny little Christmas tree on her bedside table, and I gave Ava a questioning look as we walked down the hallway as quiet as possible.

"I bought that for her last week when I wasn't sure what we were going to do Christmas-wise. I knew that even if we couldn't get a big tree for the living room, there would still be something for her."

I wrapped my arms around her and kissed her hard on the mouth, sighing into her as she pressed her hands to my chest.

"You're a good mom, Ava."

"I'm trying day by day."

We stood there for far too long, just swaying with each other to the soft sounds of Christmas carols over the speakers filling the silence. The tree was trimmed, boxes put away as much as possible, and this small cabin that was only supposed to be temporary, felt like a home.

That was Ava's doing. Sure, I'd brought over a few

boxes, and had to deal with Aaron, but it was Ava who had done this.

"You amaze me more every day," I said, not even realizing the words were out of my mouth until they were there.

She blinked up at me. "Oh?"

"Yes. You do."

"Do you want to stay for a drink? Something a little stronger than cocoa?" she asked, and I nodded.

For some reason, neither of us mentioned just being friends. We didn't mention that this was only tempo-rary. Yes, we should have, but would that be a lie?

That was the problem, wasn't it?

She made Irish cream and hot cocoa for us, and we tiptoed to her bedroom where we could talk at a normal volume with the door closed.

"We'll have to be quiet so we don't wake Faith."

I raised a brow. "What exactly are you getting me into, Ms. London?"

She blushed, her face already heated from the cocoa, and shook her head. "I meant if she hears us laughing at all, she's going to want to come investigate."

I gave a pointed look at the now-locked door. "And she'll knock?"

"Yes. I've never brought a guy home before." She frowned. "Well, she never came in without knocking when Aaron and I lived together. So there's that. And well, I don't really want to get into the details of mine and Aaron's lack of sex life."

I shuddered. "Yes. Let's not think about that ever, to be honest. I mean, it's your past, so if you need to talk about it, I'll listen, because I'm trying not to be an asshole, but I really don't want to hear it."

She shook her head as she sat down on the bed, cocoa in hand. "I don't want to talk about it either. Ever again."

"Well, I've never actually been with someone with a kid before, so you're going to have to help me down this path."

"Should we have those big conversations now?"

I took a sip of my drink, then set it down on a coaster on the nightstand. "I can't stop thinking about you or wanting you. And every time that I investigate who I want to be and the decisions I want to make, I realize that maybe I shouldn't have made a promise when I was eighteen to protect myself. And maybe in protecting myself, I'm only hurting everyone else."

She shook her head. "I don't want you to hurt yourself, or us, because you're trying to make me happy."

"You're allowed to put yourself first, you know. To want to be happy."

"I could say the same thing about you."

"No matter what happens, I'll never be Aaron," I said, putting it out there.

Her eyes widened. "I never once thought you would." Then she shook her head. "No, that's a lie."

I leaned back. "Oh?"

"I've thought to myself numerous times that I'm going down the same path. Those issues I had before— a boss who can fire me, trusting someone with such a connection to Aaron—it felt like I was making the same mistakes I already had. I'm trying not to dwell on that, only focus on what you've done, not what you could do. Which also feels shortsighted."

"So no matter what, I won't be Aaron. I'm never going to be that asshole. I'm never going to break Faith's heart."

"And what about mine?"

"I can't make any promises. But I never expected you, Ava. I never expected this."

She nodded. "I don't know what I'm supposed to think. But you're not Aaron. And I'm not the woman I was when I loved him. I don't love him anymore, in case you were worried."

Even as relief filled me, I shook my head. "Not in the slightest."

Her lips twitched because I knew she could read my mind. "So, what next?"

"Maybe we should just try this. Whatever this is. And protect Faith."

"And maybe try not to break each other's hearts in

the process," Ava said dubiously, and then I leaned forward, cupping her face in my hand.

I watched her throat work as she swallowed, and then leaned forward and took her lips with mine.

She moaned into me softly, and I knew we were going to have to be much quieter.

But she was so soft. So sweet.

I wanted her more than anything.

And maybe that should scare me. Maybe it already did.

But in the end, I just needed her.

"We have to be very quiet," she whispered against my lips, and I nodded, slowly sliding my hand down her waist to grip her hip.

"I can be quiet. But I think you're the one that's going to need to make sure that you are."

"Excuse me?" she asked, her hand sliding down my chest and between us over my jeans. I groaned, moving into her touch.

"Yes?" I asked.

"You were the one who shouted last time."

"I'm not sure I could even hear myself over your moaning."

She laughed and I took her mouth again, this time rolling so I was on top of her.

She let out a shocked gasp, moving so she could run her hands up and down my body.

This time it was slow, leisurely. All the other times had been fast and hot, and we hadn't been able to catch our breath. Even in the hotel room, we had taken each other with abandon.

And just the idea of having to be quiet added another level to it that I wasn't prepared for.

"You're so fucking beautiful," I whispered.

"Sweet talker," she said with a laugh.

I continued to explore her mouth and slowly slid my hands down her body, needing to touch her in every way possible. We stripped each other's clothes off piece by piece. When I took off her bra and her breasts fell heavy in my hands I grunted again, and she pressed her finger to my lips, reminding me to be quiet.

Oh, yes. We had to be quiet.

I took one nipple into my mouth, sucking gently, before biting down, loving the swift intake of breath between her teeth at that slight edge of pain.

"There she is."

"Wyatt."

"Keep going. That's it, crest over the edge from me just playing with your nipples."

She moaned, her hand between her thighs as I sucked on her nipples. When I put my hand over hers, cupping her so both of us inserted two fingers at the same time, she gasped at the tightness.

"That's it, help me fuck you. That's it, that's my good girl."

She shivered as I went back to her breasts, loving her taste, needing her. And when she came around our tangled fingers, knowing that she was so eager for me just pushed me on. I kissed her again before going over to the bedside table and searching for a condom.

"Better late than never," I said with a laugh, and she just shook her head at me, her eyes dark, her nipples red, her lips swollen from my attentions.

That's when I noticed the very special surprise.

"So I see you've replaced me," I said, as I pulled the vibrator out of the drawer.

She blushed, her one hand still between her thighs, the other gently playing a beat across her chest.

"I could say you could never compare, but have you seen the attachments on that thing?"

"Well, let's see what we can use this for."

It had three attachments, one for her clit, another for her ass, and the thicker part would slide into that sweet pussy of hers. I slid them on, and they made a loud noise, which made her laugh. She put her hand over her mouth, holding back the giggles.

I kept playing with the settings, until only one of them began to move.

Her eyes widened at which one I had chosen before I

turned it off again and pulled out the lube that had been next to it in her bedside drawer.

"If you're going to be that naughty on your own, it's time for you to be naughty with me."

"I think I can do that."

I gave her a quick kiss on the lips, before I popped open the lube bottle and began to work.

She writhed beneath me as I worked her hole slowly, softly, inserting one finger to the knuckle. She tightened around me, and then I pulled out, loving the way that she pouted a bit. But when I slid the vibrator deep inside, her eyes widened.

"There you go. Take it in. Let me know if I'm hurting you."

"I already feel so full."

I had my thumb over her clit, her legs spread in front of me, and I just grinned. "Oh, you're about to be full."

Her eyes widened, before they rolled back into her head when I increased the setting on the vibrator.

I angled it so it didn't hurt her, before I slid my cock against her soft and swollen folds.

"Are you ready for me?"

"Wyatt."

"That's a good girl. Take this, take me. Feel all of me. I want you to come around my cock and shout my name into a pillow. I want you to be so full that you can't tell where you are. I want to spread that beautiful pussy of yours and feel every inch wrapped around me as that vibrator fucks your ass. What do you say, babe?"

"I say I'm already ready to come."

I turned off the vibrator, and she let out a sad moan before I gently eased the tip of my cock inside her. She was so tight, and it took me a few moments to stretch her, pumping my hips softly as I slowly, ever so slowly, inch by inch, filled her.

"I've never, I've never done this," she whispered.

"It's okay. I've got you." I kissed her softly, and then I leaned back onto my knees, her legs draped over my thighs, and went to work. I turned the vibrator back on, letting it do its job in her ass, as I pressed my thumb against her clit, rolling in soft circles, and slowly worked in and out of her. Every time I moved back, her juices wetted my cock a bit further, and it was the most glorious thing I had ever seen, watching my dick disappear deep into that tight pussy of hers.

She was so fucking hot, so beautiful, and I knew that I was falling for her, even now.

I worked slow, loving the way her body began to flush, her nipples tightening, and when her body contracted, her cunt tightening around my dick, I slid the vibrator out of her ass and moved faster.

I hadn't wanted to hurt her before, but now I needed to make her beg. She wrapped her legs around my waist, but I pushed them back, needing her wide and open for me.

I pressed her thighs to the bed and pounded deep inside of her, going harder, faster, until I was forced to stop when the headboard began to shake.

I rolled us to my back, letting her take control, my hands on her breasts, squeezing her nipples just the way she wanted. She rubbed her clit against the base of my cock and kept rolling, the friction just enough, and I finally came. My balls tightened, and I sucked in a deep breath, pulling her to me so I could kiss her and muffle both of our shouts.

And when she finally draped over me, her body sweat-slick, spent, I just held her, needing to touch her.

It had never been like that before. Ever.

In all the times that I had been with others, even with her, it had never been like that.

And somehow it felt like a beginning, a beginning with her, but perhaps an ending of a path I thought I'd been forced on.

I didn't know what would happen next, I didn't know if this was the right choice, but I knew I didn't want to leave.

I knew I never wanted to leave.

Even if that was a mistake.

CHAPTER SIXTEEN
AVA

"I can't believe it's already Christmas Eve," Rory said as she nestled next to me, coffee in hand.

"I can't believe you're drinking coffee at seven at night." I teased my best friend, who I felt like I hadn't seen enough.

That morning, Faith and Wyatt and I had breakfast together, and Faith hadn't batted an eye at seeing him. I probably should have been worried about why she didn't seem fazed at all that Wyatt was there. However, she had seen him when she had gone to sleep, and when she had woken up, and we had a lovely breakfast before he had gone over to see his brothers and cousins. He would be over later as well, and I put my hand over my stomach, wondering exactly what the hell I was doing.

For someone who was trying to get her feet under her and figure out what the next phase was, I kept feeling like I was hurtling myself in far too many directions.

And yet part of me felt like maybe I should just go with it. Because every time I tried to go against it, to walk away, we kept throwing ourselves right back in.

Rory was here for a post-dinner, pre-Santa-arriving coffee apparently, just to drop off a few gifts and hang out. Once she was more settled into her new job, and both of us figured out where we were going to live full time, I knew we would see each other more often.

But until then, it was just nice to see my childhood friend.

"I like coffee," Rory said as she took a sip. "Sometimes it works wonders, sometimes it's just for flavor. Like tonight? I don't think it's going to work the way that I want it to," she said with a laugh.

"That makes sense. Of course, I'm chugging sugar again, because apparently, I'm addicted to hot cocoa."

"Hot cocoa's a thing. Faith is just drinking water now though, right?" she asked with a whisper.

I nodded as we watched Faith play with her new engineering puzzle kit Rory had brought over. "She should be going to bed soon, so Santa can come visit."

"You're Santa, Mom," Faith said with a laugh. I

winced since I hadn't known she could hear me so clearly across the house.

"Let me pretend you're my sweet little baby for a bit longer, okay?"

"Okay. Just for you." Faith went back to working on her engineering project, and I smiled.

"That little girl is brilliant. Just saying."

"Thank you for that project. That and the fancy-colored pencils so she could draw like her favorite Auntie Rory. I love it."

"Hey, I'm an illustrator. It's what I do. Now, are you going to tell me about Wyatt?" she asked, her voice so soft that I knew Faith wouldn't be able to hear over the Christmas music and the sound of her inventing.

I nearly spilled my hot cocoa over my hand and looked at my friend.

"What?"

"What? I saw him leaving. And I see the way you two look at each other. How long have you guys been sleeping together?"

"Rory," I snapped, my voice soft.

"She can't hear us."

"She literally just heard us."

"Because you were yelling, and now we are whispering."

"We're just...I don't know what we are."

Faith stood up and scampered off to the front porch since our door was open. It wasn't too cold out, and the smell of the outdoor fires from other cabins filled the air.

Faith was in her own little world, and that gave me some moments to breathe and think.

"I don't know what the two of us are. But I think we're trying something. Even though it's probably a horrible mistake."

"I'm not surprised," Rory said after a moment.

"You're not surprised about what? That it's a mistake?"

She shook her head. "No, you two always had chemistry, it's why you always fought."

I just looked at Rory, wondering what the hell she had been thinking to even say that. "There was nothing between Wyatt and me like that. Isabelle was the one who cheated on him. They were the ones together."

"You guys always had chemistry even if you didn't realize it. And he is a good man. I mean, at least from the few times I met him."

"Why did I become friends with Isabelle?" I grumbled. "Think about how our lives would've been so different if you and I had not lost touch and I never became friends with her."

"I left. I had to. But I love you. You had Isabelle, and maybe it wasn't perfect, but you had those years, just like you had those years with Aaron. It made you who you are. Don't let the mistakes of your past break into the path of your future."

"You sound like a very poorly written fortune cookie."

"Maybe. But I'm right. Those Wilders have a way of treating women right." She paused. "So I hear." I raised a brow and she shook her head. "No, I've never dated a Wilder. But I know Brooks. And if Wyatt is half the man that Brooks is, then you're in good hands."

"One day you're going to tell me that story, aren't you?" I asked, my voice soft.

"Maybe. We'll see," she said after a moment. "Anyway, I should go soon. I want to get home so Santa can visit my house."

"You can stay, you know. You don't have to celebrate alone."

"This year I do. For my own reasons. But next year? No matter where we are, it's a date."

Rory got up and said goodbye to Faith, we watched my best friend drive away, and then we settled the house down, read our favorite Christmas story before bed, and then I was tucking my daughter in.

Wyatt wouldn't be spending the night tonight, and while my body ached all over in ways it hadn't in a very long time, I was sort of glad. Tonight and first thing in the morning needed to be just about my daughter. Just about us. Adding something else too soon could be scary. But he would be here later in the morning.

And that was a step.

And as I laid my head down on the pillow that still smelled of him, I swallowed hard and wondered exactly how my life had gotten here.

The next morning Faith was up before dawn, and I wondered when those tween and teenage years came when they slept in. I was exhausted because I had tossed and turned all night, thanks to dreams of Wyatt. I sipped my coffee as Faith danced around the living room, turning on the Christmas tree lights and getting ready to open presents.

The knock at the door came far earlier than I thought it would. I looked out the peephole and saw Wyatt there, arms full of gifts, and tears pricked the back of my eyes.

"You're here early."

"Couldn't sleep. I was excited."

"Wyatt!"

"Hey there, girly." He came inside, setting the presents down on the side table before he kissed me on the cheek and picked Faith up.

"Merry Christmas," he said softly.

"Merry Christmas, Wyatt."

"Merry Christmas, Ava," he teased, and I grinned.

"Merry Christmas, Wyatt."

"Are you going to kiss Mom again?" Faith asked as she jumped to the ground and danced between us.

I froze and looked down at my daughter.

"Excuse me?"

"Oh come on, Mom. I'm not a baby. I know you two are kissing each other. And it's okay. I approve. Because he's Wyatt."

I pressed my lips together, as Wyatt blinked then grinned.

"You know what, you're right. I'm going to have to kiss your mom."

I was expecting an outrageous kiss just to make Faith laugh, but instead he cupped my cheek and slid his thumb over my cheekbone.

"Good morning, Ava."

I swallowed the hard lump of emotion in my throat. "Good morning, Wyatt."

When he brushed his lips along mine, ever so softly, I melted right then and there.

When the hell had I fallen in love with Wyatt Wilder?

And then he moved back and kissed the top of Faith's head.

"Okay, I have presents."

"Mom and I have a present for you too."

He looked over at me. "You do?"

"Just something small. You know. Maybe some coal," I teased.

Something flashed over his eyes, something warm, maybe confused? I wasn't sure, but he smiled and squeezed Faith's hand.

"I'm honored. Let's put these under the tree. I'm sorry I couldn't get them earlier. We've been a bit busy."

He was right about that. While the bar and distillery were closed today, we had been busy as all get out prepping for all the huge rushes that we had and would have for the rest of the week. People liked to party, especially between two huge holidays. And that was great for the business, and the event that Wyatt and I had gone to had made some connections to improve the business.

Things were starting to click and make sense, and I was waiting for the other shoe to drop because everything had been going so well lately.

But as I sat down next to Wyatt, both of us laughing at Faith's antics, I realized that this felt right.

Like a family.

Well, shit.

This was fine. Totally fine. But I knew I already loved him. I was just going to have to deal with that. And watching Faith move between us as if this was the most normal thing in the world, meant I needed to get my head on straight real fast.

Wyatt's phone buzzed, and I looked down to see Isabelle's name on the readout. When he scowled and hit ignore, I gave him a look.

He shook his head and mouthed later, and I wondered what that was about.

Of course, with that angry look on his face, I didn't think that he was going behind my back to see his ex-wife. Not that we had talked about being exclusive or not. We hadn't even used the R-word when it came to being in a relationship. That was something we would have to talk about though. Because I was not going to be put in the same situation I had been in with Aaron.

When Faith went to the restroom, Wyatt leaned over and kissed my cheek.

"She keeps calling to annoy me. I don't know what she wants. But I keep ignoring her."

I grimaced. "Was I that transparent?"

"My ex-wife calling on Christmas morning? Yeah, you should be transparent. No, I'm not seeing her, and I'm not seeing anyone else. It's just you, Ava. Okay? I promise."

I swallowed hard. "It's just you too. Even though I don't really know what I'm doing here."

"Honestly same. But let's figure it out together."

"Okay," I whispered, wondering how such an important conversation could happen so quickly.

And then Faith was back, and we were laughing, and

my daughter looked to be having the best time of her life.

And to think, just a couple of weeks ago I hadn't even known where I was going to lay my daughter's head to sleep at night, and now here she was, having an amazing Christmas.

And while I had something to do with it, a lot of it was thanks to the man at my side.

After we cleaned up the hoard that my daughter received, thanks to the generosity of the Wilders and our friends, Faith and Wyatt went to put together one of her new presents, and I went to the kitchen to make breakfast.

I hated putting together Christmas gifts, so if Wyatt could handle it, I would let him. I could burn eggs for the three of us.

It was my phone that rang this time, and I looked down, expecting to see my mom's name.

It still hurt to think that she wasn't going to be here for another couple of days. While the weather had warmed up nicely here thanks to being South Texas, they had been battered up north. But it wasn't my mother's name. No, it was Aaron's.

I tensed, but then remembered that maybe, just maybe, he was calling to talk to his daughter.

But not wanting to alert her or Wyatt to it, I quickly

turned the heat down on the stove and grabbed my phone, going to the front porch to answer. Wyatt gave me a look, but I waved him off, hoping he would give me a moment.

"Good morning, Aaron," I said, hoping my voice sounded steady.

"Ava."

Then he was silent for so long I didn't know what he wanted. Then again, this had to be as awkward for him as it was for me.

"Merry Christmas."

"Oh. Yeah. Uh, I have a question."

"Would you like to speak with Faith? You're more than welcome to speak with your daughter on Christmas morning. She should hear from you."

"Ava, I'm not in the mood to deal with a lecture right now."

My spine stiffened, and I realized it was going to be one of those conversations.

"It's Christmas morning. And your daughter is opening presents that have nothing to do with you. Do you even know where we live?"

"Yeah, the lawyer sent the info. I know, Ava, I sent the check for child support."

He had? I hadn't received anything, but then again, it had only been a couple of weeks since everything had happened. Odd, it felt like it had been months.

Had I really fallen in love with Wyatt Wilder that quickly?

No. But then again, I couldn't stop my heart from doing what it wanted.

Case in point: Aaron.

"If you're not calling to talk to Faith, why did you call, Aaron?"

"I was just going to see if you could wait to cash that check."

I paused, trying to understand exactly what he was asking.

"Excuse me?"

"The check that's in the mail. Wait to cash it."

"Are you serious right now? You wrote a bad check?"

"Things are happening here, Ava. You'll understand eventually. I just need you to wait a bit. Until I get some funds."

"Are you fucking kidding me? You took all our money. You took our baby's college fund. You took my retirement fund, my nest egg—everything! I barely had enough to feed our daughter and keep a roof over her head. And now you're asking me to not cash a check that is for your daughter? What the hell did you do with all that money, Aaron?"

"It's none of your fucking concern."

"If you're asking me not to spend the money that

you are legally required to send for our daughter, then it is my concern."

"You know what? Fine. Do whatever the fuck you want. I'm just saying, the money will be there eventually."

"Why isn't the money here now, Aaron?"

"Just fuck off."

"Fuck you. Merry fucking Christmas," I snapped, enraged.

When the phone went silent, I just looked down at it, my heart racing.

"Dear God," I whispered.

Aaron was such a piece of shit. He must have been that way for far longer than I knew. And yet, I hadn't realized it in time.

Thanks to my new job and this cabin, I was going to be able to feed my kid, and make sure that she had a great Christmas this morning, but what the hell was going on with my ex-husband?

It just pushed at me to make me wonder if I was making a mistake with Wyatt.

Like I had just thought, everything had happened so quickly it didn't make sense.

How could I trust him with my daughter even though I had known him for years? In fact, I had known him for as long as I had known Aaron. And I clearly hadn't known Aaron well enough. Even when we had been married.

I looked through the window as Wyatt and Faith laughed in the living room, both trying to build this drawing board setup that I would never have a chance of figuring out myself.

They looked so happy. And I knew he had always cared for Faith. But what would happen if he realized that he really didn't want children? If he walked away just like Aaron had?

But no, it wasn't fair to cast Aaron's shadow over Wyatt's light. Even if I had doubts. Even if it was perfectly logical for me to have doubts.

Something was going on with my ex-husband, and clearly something else was going on with Isabelle if she was calling Wyatt.

Was she asking for money too?

I needed to push away the pall of that phone call and celebrate this holiday morning with my daughter, because I wasn't going to have many Christmases like this left. Because one day she would be an adult and move away just like my mother and I had from each other. And we wouldn't have these moments. They were far too few and we needed to cherish them.

And yet, nothing felt right.

Everything felt too tainted.

"Ava?"

I startled, nearly dropping the phone. "Wyatt. Sorry. I didn't hear you come out."

"I gave my phone to Faith so she could call your mom. She wanted to talk to grandma. Apparently, she remembers phone numbers even though I don't," he said with a small smile. "You okay?"

I was going to say yes and lie, but instead I told him about the phone call. When Wyatt's eyes narrowed, I winced.

"I don't know what's going on with him."

"I don't know either. Maybe that's why Isabelle keeps calling? Of course, she keeps hitting on me too."

"Are you kidding me?"

He shook his head. "Not in the slightest. I don't know what the hell is going on with those two, but I guess we'll find out eventually. But none of this is going to touch Faith. You got me? I'm not going to let him hurt her. None of us Wilders are. You've got us in your corner. No matter what."

And right then I realized that he was truly different than Aaron. I needed to trust that. Even though I barely trusted myself. So in answer I put my hands on his chest and went to my tiptoes, brushing my lips against his.

"Merry Christmas, Wyatt."

He searched my face, before he nodded, a smile slowly crossing his features.

"Merry Christmas, Ava. Now, let's go see what your daughter's up to because I think she's giggling manically in there with your mother."

"She probably just told my mother that you are here for Christmas morning." I cringed. "That's going to be a fun conversation."

"Bring it on, Ava. Bring it on."

And then he took my hand and we walked inside. I had to trust this change of plans of his. And trust that he wasn't going to take that vow he had when he had been eighteen.

Because no matter what, I needed to protect my daughter.

And my heart.

CHAPTER SEVENTEEN
AVA

There was that odd time between Christmas Day and New Year's Day, where technically it was a week, only seven days, and yet your body feels like it is in this state of flux. Should you go back to work? Should you go on vacation with your family? How far are you traveling? Should you be eating more cheese? Or are you still celebrating other holidays?

Just like this week symbolized my own feelings about my current stage in life—as in I had no idea what I was doing but I was just going with the flow and perhaps wanting cheese.

A Wilder dinner.

"This is exciting," my mom said as she hugged me.

I hugged her right back, loving that my mother was finally here.

It wasn't Christmas Day, it was just a couple of days late, but exactly what I needed. My stepdad was in front of us, Faith's hand in his as they skipped along the path towards the main building.

We would be attending a Wilder family dinner in the main dining room of the inn's restaurant because they were so numerous that they needed the extra space.

I hadn't been expecting an invite, but Wyatt had casually mentioned it to my mother of all people that morning.

The introduction had gone easily, though my mother had raised a brow and given me a pointed look. I was going to have to tell her exactly what I was feeling once I figured that out.

But now we were having second Christmas and almost meet the family and parents all wrapped into one, during a time where you already felt off-kilter and wondered how time could go so fast and be stagnant simultaneously.

Somehow not only had Faith and I been invited to the Wilder dinner, or rather, been told we were going, my mother and stepfather had been as well.

So now the four of us were making our way towards the main house. It was strange to think that a snow and ice storm had not only kept my mother and stepfather away only a few days ago but had also trapped Wyatt and me in a roadside motel, but now it was so warm we didn't bother with jackets.

Texas weather was not for the weak. Or those who liked consistency.

"So, dinner with the Wilder bunch. This sounds fun."

"Mom, I don't really have answers for whatever questions you're about to ask me."

"I love that you're heading me off at the pass, as if you're afraid of what I'm going to ask, my dear child."

"I'm not truly afraid, more like wondering what I'm doing."

"Well, I'm wondering what you're doing too, but then again, it's not my place to ask." She paused, her hand falling from my shoulder to take my hand instead. "Maybe I should have asked more about Aaron. Maybe I should have seen what was right in front of me."

I shook my head. "No. You couldn't have seen if I hadn't. I mean, we didn't love each other like I thought we had, not like the way you and Daddy did. Or the way you and Pierre do."

My mom smiled. "I loved your father so much. With what I thought was everything I had. And then I realized that the heart isn't meant just to be split into two, or thirds when a baby comes along. Your heart can open and leave spaces for heartbreak, for love lost, but also for someone new in your life." She looked over at my stepdad, and I squeezed her hand right back.

"It wasn't like that for me and Aaron. I think that part just hollowed out completely. So I spackled it up and figured out how to be a single mom. And now here I am, the divorce only a little over a year final, and I'm doing it all over again."

My mom shook her head. "No, you're not. This isn't the same. And you can go as slow as you want from here on out. Yes, we're doing a family dinner where I'm meeting your beau's fourteen thousand family members." We both laughed at that. "And yes, Wyatt loves that little girl, but he always did. You can go as slow as you need to, or as fast as you want. You just need to learn to trust yourself again."

"That's the problem, isn't it? I trusted myself once, and I made one of the worst decisions of my life."

"We can both say Faith came from that decision, and you can understand that just like I can. But not every decision will turn into heartbreak. And of course, if this one does, not saying it will," she said as I raised my brows at her. "But if it does, we will come and help you bury the body. Maybe not on Wilder land because that seems like a conflict of interest, but there's a lot of land out here, honey. Some of it not even for sale. Or maybe if we do bury it on land for sale they'll have to deal with probate or whatever, you know, a bunch of lawyer terminology that I don't understand."

I rested my head on my mom's shoulders as we continued to walk, the main house in sight. "I've missed you."

"I've missed you too, baby girl. And I know living in Canada is like the furthest I could get from you and still be on the same continent it seems, but I miss you and I'm going to make sure I see you more often. We got one of those credit cards that racks up the miles. So we're going to make it happen."

"Oh yeah?"

"You know I miss my grandbaby. And from the way Wyatt looked at you this morning, I might be getting another grandbaby soon."

"Mom," I said sharply, slapping her gently on the arm.

"Don't hurt the elderly."

"Elderly my ass."

"Why are we talking about your ass?" Wyatt asked as he walked towards us, and I tripped over myself, having not realized that he was there.

"Oh. There you are." Why was my voice so squeaky?

"I didn't mean to scare you," Wyatt said as he leaned forward and kissed the side of my mouth.

I blushed, feeling awkward. I hadn't felt awkward like this since I was eighteen.

He took my hand, and I moved between him and my mother as Faith and my stepfather walked inside the main building.

We went towards the main dining room where we would be eating, and I could hear the noise from there.

"Are we late?" I asked.

Wyatt shook his head. "No, we started off with a quick founders and family meeting for business stuff. And then the kids showed up, and here we are. The only Wilder missing is Gabriel, but he'll be here for the New Year's party."

"We're having a New Year's party?" Faith asked as she skipped back over to Wyatt, who took her hand.

That sight made my heart clutch, and I swallowed hard.

"You know it. It's for the whole event and business though, so there'll be a bunch of strangers there. So we're going to have to figure out what you and your mom are doing."

He met my gaze, and I was grateful that he was trying to navigate the tricky subject of making choices for us. Because that was an invite, if not subtle.

"Could we go, Mom?" she asked, and I shook my head. But before her face could fall, I held up a hand.

"I'm not saying no even though I shook my head. It's more of a let's look at what's going on after I talk with Elliot." I looked over at Wyatt. "Elliot, right? He's the event planner?"

"Yep. My cousin and Naomi, the innkeeper, are planning it, so it'll be a big to-do with all of them. I think the kids are going, but I'm not sure," he said, warding off Faith's questions. "We'll have to ask them. Alexis will know because she's also the planner extraordinaire."

"Well, now I'm sad we're not staying for the New Year's party," my mom said, and Wyatt looked over at her.

"You can always extend your stay."

"I am meeting with my daughter's family for something right after, but we're going to plan a much longer trip next time," my stepdad said, as he moved around to hug me. I hugged him right back, inhaling that smoky scent that was just him.

Before we could make any other plans though, we entered the main room where everybody was already talking, laughing, and the wine was flowing.

"Oh, I love Wilder wine," my mom said, as Eli Wilder came forward.

"That's what we like to hear. Are you enjoying your stay so far?"

My mother put her hand to her chest as she stared at the very tall, broad, bearded Wilder, as if her husband wasn't standing right next to her.

"Oh. We love it. We just love it here. And to see my daughter? It just makes the best pairing, don't you think?"

I ignored the subtle push at that, and watched as my mother and stepfather were enveloped into the Wilder clan, and I stood back, letting Faith go to hang out with the twins and Alexis's child. Alexis had her hand on her ever-growing baby bump, and the other Wilders were all milling around, coming over to say hi, or snacking on appetizers. The dinner would be served family-style, and I couldn't believe they could do that with nine Wilders plus spouses and kids.

"Let me get you some wine," Wyatt said, as he squeezed my hand, pulling me forward.

"Is it really okay I'm here?"

"Everybody already knows we're together, and a couple of my in-laws brought their family members too. So it's fine. We're all figuring things out. My parents will be here tomorrow."

I faltered. "Oh."

"Yeah. You'll like them. And I realize I didn't give you a choice about meeting them, but they're going to be here, and I can't really hide you."

"It's amazing what happens when you say yes to one overnight, suddenly everything's moving so quickly."

We were off in the corner where hopefully no one could hear, and Wyatt let out a breath before cupping my face with both hands. I was aware that others could see us, but they couldn't hear us.

"We can slow down, I promise. But it's the holidays, and I want to see you, and I want to see my family."

"It just seems like we both changed our minds quite quickly."

"Did we? Or are we just done lying to ourselves?"

He leaned down to kiss me, and people cheered behind us but I ignored them.

"That's a good one, Wyatt Wilder."

"You just like saying my name, don't you?"

"They both start with Ws. It's fun to say."

"At least I don't start with an E like the rest of them."

"Excuse me, I'm hearing you making fun of me?" Elliot Wilder said. "By the way, we have a full staff for the New Year's party, so you're so invited. I thought you already had been because you worked for us, and you're with Wyatt, but in case you didn't get the memo, you're invited. Faith's invited. All of you are invited. And we have childcare. So don't worry. Dance all night to your heart's content. And maybe we'll get Lark and Gabriel to sing."

"What are you making my wife do?" East called from the other side of the room.

"I'll sing, though you have to get Gabriel off his bum to do so," Lark said with a laugh.

"That would be fun," I said with a smile, but Wyatt didn't say anything and I had to wonder what that was about. Only I'd ask him in private since I knew he was worried about his brother.

As Elliot went off, leaving Wyatt and me alone, Wyatt poured a glass of wine and handed it to me.

"We okay?" His voice was gruff then, and I swallowed hard, grateful for the wine to keep my mouth busy as I thought my answer over.

"Oddly, I think we are. But the whole not lying to ourselves anymore? That's going to take a minute for me to get used to. Sometimes I like sitting in my own denial. It keeps me safe."

His lips twitched but then he nodded. "As someone who was married to the wrong woman for far too long, I'm with you there." We clinked glasses, and he kissed me again. I ignored the knowing gazes as we went over to sit next to Faith, who was happily sitting next to Brooks, the two of them in a deep conversation about some animated cartoon. I left them at it, and we ate some of the most delicious food ever. I was going to have to add in an actual workout to my day thanks to all the Wilder food. And it had nothing to do with just the holidays.

By the time we were done, it was getting late and I walked my mother, stepfather, and Faith back to the pink cabin.

"Hey, I need to head into the office to do a few things and set up for tomorrow. Do you mind if I come back later tonight?"

"You go off and have fun," my mom said, obviously overhearing.

I rolled my eyes at her and looked at Wyatt. "How about I go tuck Faith in, and then I head over to you? I'll help you with that paperwork so you can get off early, and then we can watch a movie or something."

"I'd rather get off with you," he whispered in my ear, and I blushed. My mother laughed, and I had a feeling that she heard that. Blushing even harder, I shoved at his chest.

"You're a dork."

"Yes, but I'm your dork," he said with a laugh.

"Too much wine, Wilder!"

"That's why I'm walking," he said with a laugh.

I shook my head and followed my mother towards my cabin.

I ignored their knowing looks and teases, and tucked Faith in, grateful that she was exhausted after a long day. School would be starting soon, and I was as excited as her about this one. Alexis and Kendall had already done tons of research for their children even though they weren't the same age, so that meant that we were all set, even though we had changed out of the blue in the middle of the school year.

Things were going well. Finally.

Even though we had gotten that crazy phone call from Aaron a few days ago, nothing else had come of it.

I was happy.

Even stressed, worried, and ever-changing, I was happy.

And what an odd thing to be.

Leaving my mother and stepfather watching Faith, I hopped in a golf cart, since I only had one glass of wine, and drove towards the distillery and bar. I wanted to help Wyatt so he wouldn't have to work too late. And no, it wasn't just so I could make out with him in the office. That would be a perk though.

It was crazy to think how much I loved working for him. Yes, he was technically my boss, but we worked well together. There was the whole distillery section and I felt like I was learning so much from Sam. He was brilliant, and watching him work made me want to do better. And Wyatt was personable, a great manager, and a kick-ass bartender. I didn't have to work too many bartending shifts because he needed me in the manager position, but I was helping.

And while I thought possibly this would be temporary, maybe it could be more. Maybe I could help the Wilders thrive like they wanted to.

I pulled into one of the reserved parking spaces for the golf carts and used my key to walk inside.

Wyatt had music going, not too loudly, and I smiled, content for the first time in a long time.

Then my heart leapt into my throat as I saw Wyatt wasn't alone at the bar.

Instead, he leaned against it, his hands on the hips of another woman, and Isabelle plastered to him, her lips an inch from his.

CHAPTER EIGHTEEN
WYATT

I checked the clock hanging over the bar, hoping that I wasn't going to be here too much longer. I wanted to go back to Ava's place and watch a movie, even though her parents and daughter would be there. But I didn't mind. It was odd that it just felt so right. After years of denying that I might want something more than what I had, here I was, going all in.

Apparently, all it took was a spark, an ice storm, and a little girl telling you that she loved you for you to fall.

I had spent so long denying that I could have more, that I hadn't even considered the possibility.

I didn't know if I wanted more kids, or if maybe Faith was the exception to the rule, and that was something that I would have to work out, but I liked being with Ava.

I liked that we either fought or got along, and there was no in-between. I liked that she made me smile and try to be better.

I liked that she was making this place shine, and I hadn't even realized something was lacking until she showed up.

It was all supposed to be temporary, her and I, her working here, her being here. Now I didn't want her to go.

Well, hell. Was that love? I had been in love before. At least, I thought I had been with Isabelle. And while that had turned out like the fiery depths of hell, it wasn't the be all, end all. Maybe this was completely different.

I rubbed my hand over my chest, frowning. It *was* completely different.

Holy hell, I was in love with Ava London.

That sounded like something I should probably tell her, but was it too fast? Or was it something that I had been missing all along?

A little dazed, I went back to my paperwork that I had spread all over the bar. Every time I was in the office these days, I thought about Ava, and it was hard to think with a hard-on. So I wanted to finish a couple of things that needed to be done out here where I could think, and then I would head back to Ava's with her, because she should be here any moment now.

And as if I had conjured her, there was a knock at the front door.

She had a key to the back door, but maybe she had wanted to come up front, though I was still on alert because for some reason the hairs on the back of my neck stood on end.

I looked at the cameras, just in case, remembering the last time I had been here alone and someone had come through the front door.

But it wasn't Ava.

And it wasn't some man out there trying to steal my money bag and beat the shit out of me.

What the hell was my ex-wife doing out there?

And while I could just ignore her, she would make a racket and probably annoy any guests that might be about.

It was lucky that we had closed early today for my staff to enjoy some of their holiday, or she could have just walked right in.

But I couldn't leave her out there; even though it wasn't freezing, she would still annoy the hell out of whoever was around, and that was bad for business. And frankly, I wanted to get this over with. Aaron apparently needed money, so what did Isabelle want?

I just needed to get this over with, figure out exactly what the hell she wanted, and get her gone. Completely.

Of course, if she remained with Aaron, and Ava and I continued this path we were on, Isabelle was never going to be out of our lives. Because Faith would always connect us. But in the end, that didn't matter. Because Faith and Ava were what came first.

I undid the locks and opened the door, wanting to get this over with.

"Isabelle, we're closed."

"Oh, even for me?" she teased.

"Especially for you," I growled, the thought of having to deal with her more than this moment annoying the hell out of me.

"You always were a jerk sometimes, but I forgive you."

"I don't have time for any of your games, Isabelle. Is there something wrong? Why are you here?"

She looked around the empty bar and distillery—the thing that I hadn't even realized had been my dream until I was living it.

I was proud of this place, about what we'd put into it. I knew we still had a long way to go and that we would forever be finding ways to expand, or even enhance what we already had. But when I looked at the gleaming wood and small touches that made this place a home to me, I realized that I had everything I wanted. And hadn't even realized what that meant until now.

I didn't want to see the place that I loved in the eyes of the woman I thought I had loved at one time.

"Why are you closed so early on a weeknight? I didn't realize that you guys were having such downtime."

"It's the holidays, and you know it. So either you're going to continue to hit on me inappropriately, or you're going to put down my place. You can't really do both and still get whatever the fuck you want. So, why are you here, Isabelle? Get it over with, and then get out of here. I'm not in the mood to deal with whatever's going on in your mind right now."

Her eyes look sad, and I recognized in that moment the Isabelle I had married. Not the sadness but the realness. Somewhere along the way, as our lives had changed, she had lost that. And I hadn't even realized it until it was too late.

"I love Aaron. He's going to be my husband. And we're going to have the life that we've always dreamed of."

It wasn't a kick in the gut to hear that. If anything, it was almost relief. Because maybe they would just get the hell out of town. As much as it burned me to think it, Faith was better without Aaron. At least for now. Until he could get his selfish ass in the right mindset to be a father.

Although, that wasn't my right to say; I didn't have a voice in this situation.

"That's good. So, why are you here, Isabelle?"

"I just want to talk. About, you know, old times."

I frowned, looking at her, studying her face. Something was off about this. I didn't know what it was, but she might have wanted me just to fuck with me, or even to fuck me. But she didn't really want me.

Something else was going on here and I had no idea what.

What the hell did she want?

"I've missed you," she whispered, and then she pushed me back against the bar, her hand on my chest, and I leaned back, trying to keep as far from her as I could.

"Isabelle, what the hell?" And when her lips pressed to mine, I froze, knowing I couldn't hit a woman or push her down, but what the fuck?

"Excuse me?" a voice said from the back door, and I turned my head, finally able to gently nudge Isabelle away.

"Ava, it's not what it looks like."

This was one of my worst nightmares. I had no idea what Isabelle was doing there, and of course Ava was here. She had said she would come here. And this was what she saw? After so long of her not being able to trust people because of what Aaron and

Isabelle did, and here it was happening again. Oh hell no.

I opened my mouth to say something else as Isabelle smirked, but Ava just shook her head.

My heart fell, my stomach twisting.

"Ava, I promise it's not what it looks like."

Ava moved forward and tapped Isabelle's shoulder. "He might not be able to touch you because you'll cry to your boyfriend, fiancé, or whatever the hell you're calling Aaron these days. Or you'll call the cops. I know you, Isabelle. I might not trust you, but I know your type now. I don't care what you think you can do to me. You've already done it. Don't touch him."

Flabbergasted, I just stood there as Isabelle took a few steps back and smirked. "Oh, so I guess the rumors are true. You did open your legs for him."

"Are you fucking kidding me?" I snapped.

Ava just gave me a look before glaring at Isabelle. "And? I was single. You made sure of that, didn't you? You need to go."

"Wyatt, aren't you going to stop her from talking to me this way?"

I threw my head back and laughed, wrapping one arm around Ava's waist.

"You've never listened to me. So no, I'm not going to stop her from telling you the truth. Ava doesn't listen to me either, but that's different. It's how we like it." I gave her a wink and Ava rolled her eyes before glaring back at Isabelle.

"Fuck you, Wyatt," Ava whispered, and I snorted.

"Later," I said with a laugh.

I still didn't know why Isabelle was here. But standing next to Ava where everything felt as if it made sense? Hell, I really did love this woman. It was about time I told her.

"Go home, Isabelle. You're not wanted here. You're just making a fool of yourself."

"Aaron is still Faith's daddy. You can't keep us away."

For an instant, Ava looked as if she had been slapped at the reminder, but I was the one who leaned forward. Anger coursed through me as I glared at my ex-wife. "Don't, don't bring him into this."

"I can handle this," Ava said.

"You did. To protect me. Now it's my turn." I turned back to Isabelle. "Go away. You can play all the games you want with me, and I'm not going to budge, but you hurt that kid? You even talk about her? You'll have to deal with me."

"You're such a fucking bastard," Isabelle said, her true colors coming to light. "Why couldn't you just stay distracted?"

I wondered what the hell she was talking about,

until footsteps sounded from behind me. I turned, putting my body between whoever it was and Ava.

Aaron stood there with a fucking knife in his hand, looking pissed as hell. "Aaron?"

I ignored Ava's words, realizing that Isabelle was behind us now, and all of this had been a setup. But for what?

"What are you going to do with that knife, buddy? What are you doing here, Aaron?"

"Why can't you just for once do what you're supposed to?" Aaron snapped.

"I'll get the register. You get the bags?" Isabelle said, and everything began to click into place.

Isabelle's taunts, her reaching out. That might have been to just fuck with me, but also because she wanted to distract me.

From Aaron.

"It was you who attacked me that one night. It was right after you left, but I never thought you would've been the one to do it."

"You know, I was honestly pleased to see that the cops and you thought it was that one rancher. But hell, he might've been doing the other places. I'm not a robber, I don't usually do things like that. We just needed a few bucks."

Isabelle rummaged around, and I didn't know if she

was armed, but I couldn't keep my eyes off Aaron, not with the knife in his hand and Ava right by my side.

"Aaron, what are you doing?" Ava asked, her voice soft.

"Doing what I need to. I've got debts, bills to pay. And Wyatt always had everything he's ever wanted. He has enough to share, but he never did. Isabelle didn't get enough in the divorce. So now I am taking what was rightfully ours to begin with."

"Just put the knife down, man. We can talk this through."

"No, we can't. First, you weren't supposed to be here, and then Isabelle was supposed to distract you once we realized you were, but I didn't know my fucking ex-wife was going to be here to ruin it all. I just need a few dollars to pay off the bookie and then I'll be done."

"You're gambling again?" Ava asked, and I blinked at my former best friend.

"How much debt are you in?" I asked, my voice a rasp. I didn't know how we were going to get out of this, but I would find a way. Ava was not going to get hurt by this man again.

"Fuck off," he snapped as he came closer, knife outstretched.

"Don't," I said, my hands in front of me. "Take what you need and get out."

"So you can call the cops? I don't think so."

Ice slid down my spine as I realized that Aaron didn't have a way out of this either, because he was on camera and the cops were going to figure this out no matter what.

"Just go. We're not going to call them," I said, not even knowing if that was a lie.

"I can't get the fucking register open," Isabelle snapped.

"There's no money in that, anyway," Ava said. "It's after closing, but I'll get you what you need and then you just go, okay?"

"You left him such a mess and now he must pay you every month for that fucking brat, and all I wanted was to have the man of my dreams and relax. But no, why do you ruin everything?"

I would deal with the fact that she had just called Faith a brat later, but first, I had to focus on the fact that Aaron was coming closer, waving that knife around.

"Here, I'll get you the money," I said bending down towards the safe. Aaron lurched at that, as if I had moved too quickly. Ava shouted, turning to move towards Isabelle, but I had to focus on the knife coming towards me. I ducked to the right, the knife slicing across my arm. Fiery pain shot up as it sliced the skin, but I moved quickly before it could go any deeper.

Isabelle screamed behind me, and I had to hope that Ava had her down. Isabelle wasn't armed, so I needed to get the knife out of Aaron's hand.

"You bastard!" Aaron shouted as he came at me again, so I did the one thing I could that I knew would take him down. I kneed my former best friend in the nuts and then used my fist in a right hook. It wasn't pretty, and I wasn't a fighter, and I didn't know what the fuck I was doing like my brothers would have, but as Aaron hit the ground, the knife clattering across the tile floor, I put my knee to his back and pinned him down.

"Ava," I said, looking up at her, who had Isabelle on the ground as well, her arms behind her.

"Holy hell," Ava exclaimed. "Are you okay? You're bleeding."

"I'm fine," I said, hoping that was true. "You?"

"She pulled my hair and might've scratched my neck," she said, tilting so I could see the four red marks along her neck. "I hope I don't get rabies."

"I fucking love you," I blurted. Ava's eyes widened and I realized what I just said.

She smiled at me as adrenaline coursed through us both.

"I love you too. But right now I need to figure out how to get to a phone but keep her down."

"You fucking whore!" Isabelle screamed and began

to thrash, but Ava had her down. Aaron continued to wail, his body shuddering in sobs as the reality of the situation hit him. I pulled my phone from my back pocket and called Ridge, knowing he would figure out what to do.

But I hadn't needed to call, because my brother slammed through the door, his phone ringing from his back pocket as he ran towards us.

"Sorry I'm late. I was on the other side of the fucking compound. But we saw everything on the security systems, and the police are on their way."

"Bastard!" Isabelle began to scream, but I ignored her as my brother and his team came in, the cops following soon after. And then my arms were open, and Ava was running towards me, throwing herself at me.

"You could have died," she whispered, kissing my chin, then my lips.

I wrapped my arms around her, ignoring the wince as my arm throbbed with pain.

"All I could think about was keeping you safe."

"I love you, even though I sort of screamed it back, I love you."

My lips twitched and I kissed her again. "I love you too. We'll figure out the rest soon, okay? Everything. But first, I think I'm going to need to sit down. Because the adrenaline crash? That's fucking real."

Her eyes widened, as she moved to the side, still

cradled between my legs as I sat on the bar stool and the paramedics came over to look at my arm.

I didn't know what was going to happen next. What would happen to both of our exes. But Faith was safe with her grandparents in the cabin, and the woman I loved was in my arms.

We would figure out what to do later, and what it all meant. But I didn't let Ava go, not even when Ridge glared at me for not calling as soon as Isabelle had shown up.

It wasn't as if I could've known that my ex-wife was also part of the attack from before. No, it was my former best friend who had attacked me and left me for dead. And then tried to do it again.

I would have to come to terms with that later, but for now I just held Ava, knowing that this was right. Given the chaos of everything that was wrong, Ava in my arms was right.

And I would cling to that.

Because she was a choice I hadn't even realized I could make. She was everything, my everything.

I let out a breath and let the paramedics work.

Ava cupped my face and glared at me. "Never get nearly stabbed again."

My lips twitched as the paramedics snorted beside us.

"I will do my best."

"No, you're going to have to do better than your best. Because this has been a very eventful month and we're starting a new year. So no more stabbings, no more break-ins. No more exes. Just happy things."

I leaned down and kissed her again. "Okay. That I promise."

After all, we only had a few days left of the year, but I wasn't going to ask what else could happen. I wasn't that dumb.

I just held Ava and hoped to hell things would calm down. Although, with the woman that I once thought I hated in my arms, maybe calm wasn't going to happen. Yet I didn't think I was going to mind. Not with Ava and Faith as part of a future I hadn't even realized I needed.

CHAPTER NINETEEN
WYATT

"Am I really allowed to stay up until midnight?" Faith asked, and I looked over at Ava because I shouldn't be the one to answer this question.

I was still Wyatt, and sometimes Uncle Wyatt to Faith, but we were not at the point yet where I got to make major decisions like letting an eight-year-old stay up until midnight for the new year so we could watch the ball drop on the East Coast. Okay, that meant we would stay up until eleven, and then the kids would hopefully go to sleep, and then we'd have ten minutes or so just to ourselves to ring in the new year. It wasn't how I used to spend my New Year's, but it was something. And I wouldn't change it for anything.

"Yes. But then you must go to sleep, along with the

Wilder cousins. If you don't, then I get cranky. And you know how you hate it when I'm cranky."

"Okay, and then tomorrow are we going on the five-mile thingy?"

I shuddered and looked at Ava, who just laughed.

"I am not going on the 5K," I said slowly. "Brooks is welcome to do that, but I think he was just joking. There is a 5K next week that we can still sign up for if you want to."

"Do I have to run the whole time?" Faith asked.

I shook my head. "Nope. Not even when people are screaming on the sidelines for you to keep going and to run. We can walk the whole way."

"Excuse me, what is this we you're talking about?" Ava asked. "I do not run. 5Ks sound exhausting."

"We can do it, Mom."

"That's something the two of you can do with the Wilders. I will be sitting on the sidelines with water when you guys are done. And maybe a cookie."

"Wait, I get cookies? I'm in," Faith said.

"The cookie was for me, but I suppose I could share," Ava said, and then Faith ran to her mom, and the two of them sat on the couch, laughing and wrestling with one another.

I pulled out my phone and snapped a photo, knowing that Ava might want that. Of course, one of the angles on the photo made her eyes look crossed, but I would keep that. Maybe frame it.

That's what happened when you were in love, you took those moments that you never thought possible and kept them forever.

It was odd to think that from one morning of me craving eggs, that now I was here, watching the love of my life laughing with Faith in her arms. And that I'd be running a 5K the next week. Oh, I'd be walking part of it, but Faith had already done some club sports, and we were going to enroll her in new ones starting this semester. I was going to do my best to find all the best things for her so she never felt like she was lacking. Aaron had already done a number on this family, and I wasn't going to let it happen again.

Aaron was out of jail. But he was probably going to end up either serving some time or doing a shit-ton of community service and probation. I wasn't sure what I wanted, but if Faith didn't feel as if her little heart was breaking because of what Aaron had done? I didn't care what happened to the man.

We were never going to recover the money that Aaron stole and used to pay his gambling debts, but that was fine with me. A small part of me still felt as if I would've done anything for Aaron if he had reached out for help.

If he had reached out any time during those years

that he had been floundering, I would've done something for him. Yes, he had already broken Ava and Faith's hearts by then, but the small part that had once been my best friend? That part I wouldn't have wanted to fail. Even if he had been with Isabelle.

I didn't know how their relationship was going to go, or even if they were still together. I didn't care. I might hear about it through the grapevine that was South Texas at some point, but in the end there was nothing I needed to do or could do about Aaron.

He was always going to be Faith's biological father, but we were in the process of seeing if Aaron wanted to give up custodial rights. If only to protect Faith and her assets in the future.

Faith didn't ever talk about her father, at least not in front of me. And from what Ava had been telling me, she didn't mention him to her either. Starting at the end of the month Faith would be going to therapy, thankfully covered by the insurance the Wilders' company provided. And Ava would be going as well.

I didn't know if I would ever be invited, and I'd be fine if not. Talking about my feelings outside of my family and Ava really wasn't my thing. Hell, it sounded as fun as pulling teeth. However, if Faith needed me there, I'd be there.

I loved that kid as if she were my own. And maybe one

day she would be. But that was going too far, too fast, especially because I knew we all needed some time figuring out this phase of our life before we moved on to the next.

"I'm going to go get on my dress. Can I?" Faith asked, and Ava and I looked at each other before Ava nodded.

"Go for it. I'm going to put on mine soon too."

I held back a groan at the thought of Ava in that sparkly little dress, while the woman that I loved just gave me a pointed look.

Yeah, maybe getting a hard-on and groaning at the thought of Ava in a very small dress that I could ruck up over her hips and fuck her from behind in wasn't the thing to be thinking about right now.

And hell, there went that image.

I turned towards the fridge to look inside for something, even though I didn't need anything, and Ava let out a small laugh.

Damn that woman, she knew exactly what she did to me.

Faith and Ava went to get ready, and I did the same, though I was just going to be wearing jeans and a Henley. At least it was dark jeans and a dark gray Henley, but I wanted to be comfortable. Ava came out in that sparkly dress of hers that shimmered at her thighs, and a wrap of some sort that covered her arms and wouldn't really keep her warm. Of course, that was going to be my job tonight.

At that thought, I moved forward and took her by the chin, kissing her softly on the lips.

"Hey there."

"Hi. That's a nice way to say hello."

"You look beautiful."

"This was in one of the boxes you brought over. I'm so grateful that you did."

"The dress looks great, and I'm glad I found it, but it's not what makes you beautiful."

"You're ridiculous," she said with a laugh.

"Maybe, but I love you. Just want to make sure you knew that."

Her eyes shone again as she kissed me hard on the mouth, reaching around to squeeze my ass.

I laughed as Faith skipped in wearing bright purple sparkly Mary Janes, and a sparkly dress to match.

"What's so funny?" Faith asked. "Kissing isn't funny, right? Because I like it when you guys kiss. It makes me feel all warm inside." She wrapped her arms around both of us, and I met Ava's gaze, completely at a loss for what to do here.

I had never dealt with children like this before. And I had no idea what I was supposed to do.

Ava took charge so I didn't have to worry.

"Kissing can be funny. I just like being with Wyatt, so it makes me laugh and smile."

"Good," Faith said with a firm nod. "I like it when you smile. You need to do it more often."

I grinned at Ava, who sighed. "Yes, well, Wyatt does know how to make me laugh. Come on now. Let's get your coat and head over to the main building with the Wilders. Are you ready to party?"

"Always. Gabriel said he was going to show me how to do the two-step."

"Your brother knows how to do the two-step?" Ava asked incredulously.

I cringed. "I have no idea. But if he doesn't know, rockstar brother that he is, I'm pretty sure that Elliot knows."

"I love Elliot. He's dreamy. And his husband and wife are dreamy too. Can I have a husband and wife too when I get older? That way I don't have to choose. I like that he gets to have more than one. It just seems right."

I held back my laughter as Ava gently nudged Faith towards the golf cart that we were going to take to the main building.

"If that's what you want, we will love you either way. In fact, we'll love you no matter who you marry as long as they love you back. Or even if you never get married at all."

"I know that. You and Wyatt love me no matter what. Duh."

She said that with such conviction that I nearly tripped over my feet. But I got in the golf cart, made sure both of my women were buckled in, and drove towards the inn.

With all that Aaron had done to this family, his daughter still believed in me.

It was going to take everything within me to make sure I didn't fuck that up. Ava deserved the world. Faith deserved even more.

We pulled up to the main building, where guests and family members were mingling, the party already in full swing. The innkeeper Naomi had worked hard with Elliot to make sure that the place was decked to the nines and looked amazing. Plus there was food and drinks and safe spaces for people to find quiet as well. It really was something out of this world, and I couldn't believe that my family had done this. That we were all together, somehow making it work.

Faith hugged us tightly, then ran off toward Alexis and Eli to go play with the younger kids. There were also children her age at the event, and they all mingled together, with nannies and babysitters watching. Of course, there were always going to be Wilder eyes on them as well.

That was just the name of the game.

Ridge and Aurora were the first ones to greet us, and I hugged my future sister-in-law tight.

"You're looking happy."

"I feel happy. I love the way you guys celebrate holidays. Not only did I get to make a bunch of desserts that I've always wanted to make, including various petit fours—"

"Did you say petit fours?" I pounced on her words.

"Yes, and if the horde of children and Wilders haven't gotten to them already, there should be some left for you. If not, I did save some in the walk-in refrigerator for you, but be sneaky. Only you and Ridge know."

"I knew I was your favorite Wilder," I said as I kissed her temple.

"Watch yourself with my woman," Ridge grumbled, his arm around Ava.

Both Ava and Aurora gave each other looks before bursting into laughter.

"Yes, because the 'my woman' thing really works when you're holding my woman," I drawled.

"What? I'm a caveman. Sue me. However, we will have to keep the petit fours between us," Ridge whispered.

"Did someone say cake?" Brooks said as he came forward, his plate piled with food.

I blinked at him and the wild assortment of appetizers on this plate.

"Did you save some for anyone else?" I asked, before I reached forward and plucked a quiche off his plate and popped it into my mouth.

Brooks glared at me, but then Ridge did the same thing, and my brother realized it was a lost cause.

He held out his plates, and both Ava and Aurora plucked different appetizers for themselves—a bacon pinwheel for Ava and a broccoli cheddar pastry thing for Aurora.

"Why do I even bother trying to feed myself? You guys just take from me every day."

"Oh, shut up," Ridge and I said at the same time before grinning.

"You act like the put-upon older brother when I am the eldest here," Ridge put in.

"Well, I'm second eldest."

"And I'm the perpetual middle child." I paused, looking around the group. "Where's the baby of the family?" I asked.

"He was off in the back talking with one of the caterers." Ridge rolled his eyes. "I don't want to know what he's up to."

I winced. "Well, that's going to be annoying. But he's a rockstar, guess he must live up to the reputation."

"Or he can settle down," Aurora said, and winced. "Well, doesn't that sound presumptuous of me? Pretend I didn't say that. However, maybe we could set him up."

Ava tapped her chin. "But with who? Rory is the only friend I have here outside of the Wilders, which is a sad state, but I have good friends here."

"Rory? Oh, she's beautiful. And smart."

"She really is."

"Okay you guys, if you could stop trying to set up our baby brother with your friends, that would be great."

"I might have a couple friends in the baking business too."

"Oh, we should take some notes." Then both women looked at Brooks. "And you know, someone could be good for you."

Brooks coughed on his mushroom tartlet and shook his head. "No, thank you. Seriously. No thank you. Rory and I would never get along."

I met Brooks's gaze as he changed the subject to Gabriel's new single, and then looked over at Ridge.

We knew that Brooks had dated since losing his wife, though not anything seriously. But wasn't it interesting that he mentioned Rory of all people? Considering that Aurora had brought up some of her friends as well. I hadn't forgotten that odd interaction when I had first met the other woman. Of course, I could just be thinking along those lines because I had Ava in my arms, now that Aurora had gone to Ridge's side.

We mingled about with the others, making sure that we had eyes on Faith the entire time. She seemed to be having an amazing time and we ended up dancing, Ridge teaching Faith the two-step as Gabriel was nowhere to be found. I needed to find my brother, but every time I tried to, I got distracted by a million other things, including the gorgeous woman in my arms.

And when the East Coast clock struck midnight, we began our first round of 'Happy New Year's, before the kids were tucked into bed upstairs in the inn, and then I held the woman of my dreams in my arms and wondered how I had gotten so lucky.

"So, did you ever think we'd be here?" I asked as the clock began to count down again.

"Never. But I don't mind it. You are kind of cute."

"I try." I winked. "This starts a brand-new year. A clean slate."

Ava shook her head. "No. I need the jagged parts a bit longer. To remind me where we came from. And where I want to go."

I swallowed hard and nodded, understanding. "Okay, so no clean slates, how about a new beginning?" I asked, feeling like a fool. I wasn't good at words; I wasn't good at figuring out what I was supposed to say in the moment. But right then and there, I knew I had to say something.

Ten.

Nine.

"I love you, Ava."

Eight.

Seven.

"I love you, Wyatt Wilder."

Six.

Five.

My heart picked up a beat. "Yeah?"

A nod.

Four.

Three.

"And I can't wait to fuck you in this dress," I groaned into her ear.

Two.

One.

And I caught Ava's laugh with my lips.

As everyone cheered on the new year, I slid my arms around Ava, grabbing her ass. There were too many people for them to notice what we were doing, so I just kissed her, and when she pulled back, her eyes had darkened.

"You know I was going to say you looked hot as hell in that Henley. There's just something about a man that shows off his forearms. You little tease."

I threw my head back and laughed, and then kissed her again as the world celebrated the new year, the coming change and everything that came with it, and I held the woman that I loved and knew this was only our beginning.

We had forever in front of us, even if we hadn't realized it at the time.

There was far more to come, and nothing could ever be perfect, but in this moment, it felt perfect.

In this moment, I had the woman I thought I had hated, the woman I thought I had needed to save, but in the end had saved me.

I had my Ava. My family. My forever.

CHAPTER TWENTY
GABRIEL

The whiskey slid down my throat, smooth with a fiery edge. I looked down at the low-ball glass in my hand, and the large ice cube shaped like a skull, and snorted. I had never been a whiskey guy, or a liquor guy. I had always liked cheap beer, anything out of a keg, and maybe even some wine that my cousins made. But these days, the harder the better. I needed that burn.

Funny that I even craved any of that considering I didn't drink much these days. I couldn't drink while out on tour. I didn't want to. I needed to be sharp. I don't think people realized how much it took me to just focus on a regular basis.

I had to be on the top of my game to stay where I was, and I didn't even know where I was at this point.

Such an odd thing to think, considering that's not what I thought my life would be.

I took another sip of the whiskey, hoping it would help me forget.

Forget.

How odd, since that was the title of my number one song right now. And yet there was nothing I could do to scrape those memories from my subconscious. There was nothing I could do to forget. The drink wasn't going to help, so I wasn't going to go too far.

I always had to control myself, because if I went too far, I knew there would be no coming back.

I had seen what happened when other people went too far. I had held them in my arms as they faded away and lost themselves to the oblivion they thought they craved.

I wasn't going to let myself fall again.

And yet sometimes it felt like all I was doing was falling. My fingers gripping at the edge of the abyss as there was nothing left for me.

I took another sip of the whiskey. This time it didn't burn.

Should that bother me?

Yeah, that should really bother me.

There was a laugh out in the distance, and I looked across the stone parkway at my brother as he twirled his fiancée in his arms. Aurora had her head back, her hair flowing as she danced with Ridge.

It was good to see those two together. After everything Ridge had lost, he deserved that.

Though it broke me that I hadn't even known he had lost anything.

That none of us had.

That kind of loss broke a man, and Ridge had been broken. Then again, Aurora had lost everything as well and here they were, finding their way to each other.

So weird how that happened. That it could happen. It almost made me believe in happy ever afters.

Though we all knew I didn't.

I pulled my jealous gaze from Ridge and Aurora, and sadly it went right to Wyatt.

It was nearly eleven now, our family partying for the new year, cousins and nieces and nephews running about, and Wyatt stood there, holding eight-year-old Faith in his arms as she laughed at something he said as if it was the most hilarious thing in the world.

My brother, a father.

That didn't even make sense to me.

Yet, it was there.

The way that he cared for Faith, and the way that Ava stood back, her phone in hand as she took photo after photo. The three of them fit together. As if they had been meant to be a family all along but had taken a few bumps and turns along the way.

I didn't know how they could make that connection, that they could bury the past and find their future, but I was grateful for it. It just didn't make sense to me how they could even find that.

But what did I know?

I was alone. Something I was damn good at.

It was weird that you could be alone when thousands of people were screaming your name, begging for you to be inside them physically and emotionally.

But no, that wasn't me.

Someone came to my side, and I looked over at Brooks, a bottle of the same whiskey I was currently drinking in his hand. He had a low-ball glass in his other hand and raised a brow in question.

"More?"

I held out my glass without saying a word.

The sound of liquid pouring over ice filled the quiet, even over the din of music and cheering from my family.

I nodded in thanks and took a sip, Brooks taking a sip of his own.

"Never thought I'd see you out here drinking."

I looked over at my brother. "Are we really going to have a talk right now?"

"Are you really going to be an asshole?" Brooks asked.

"I am an asshole. It's what I'm good at."

Brooks just shook his head. "I know why I am out here. You know why I'm out here, but why the hell are you, Gabe?"

"I'm fine. I'm just relaxing before I go on tour."

"I'm on my first drink. How many does that make for you?" he asked.

I swallowed hard, then took a sip of my whiskey, not answering.

I wasn't going to get drunk. Just buzzed. Then I would stop drinking so I could focus on the tour.

I could run miles and miles on the treadmill, singing my heart out to the songs that I had put my heart into. I could swim for laps and laps, and I could lift like nobody's business.

I was strong, I was healthy, but I just wanted to be numb. I didn't want to feel anything. Why couldn't anyone believe me when I said that?

"I'm here when you want to talk."

I looked at my brother and knew that everything that I had gone through might've cut me deep, but it was nothing compared to Brooks. And I had to remember that. I just wrote songs for a living. I needed to be grateful.

"I know," I said softly.

Brooks stood there for a moment and then walked back to the family, taking the bottle with him. I didn't know if it was for his own good, or mine, but I should be grateful.

When the clock finally struck midnight and everyone cheered, I stood in the shadows and kept drinking.

Because if I kept doing this, then the numbness would remain. If only for the night.

It wasn't like the music would ever leave, because it always screamed. Even when I slept.

Happy fucking New Year.

Reality would settle in. And I'd have to make a choice.

One I didn't know if I'd ever be ready to make.

NEXT IN THE WILDER BROTHERS SERIES:
Gabriel and Briar find out their path in PIECES
OF ME.

IF YOU'D LIKE TO READ A BONUS SCENE
FEATURING AURORA & RIDGE:
CHECK OUT THIS SPECIAL EPILOGUE!

A NOTE FROM CARRIE ANN RYAN

Thank you so much for reading **Forever for Us!**

I'll be honest. This is one of my favorite books I've written in a long time. Wyatt and Ava burned the pages and I couldn't wait to sit down and write their HEA. I hope you loved their story as much as I did.

Next up? I get to write the romance I've been waiting for since I first came up with the Wilders. Gabriel's life is about to be...rocked. And I'm so freaking excited for you to read their romance!

If you'd like to start at the beginning of the series, Eli and Alexis start everything with One Way Back to Me.

If you'd like to read Eliza Wilder's story, you can find it in Inked Obsession!

The Wilder Brothers Series:

Book 1: One Way Back to Me (Eli & Alexis)

Book 2: Always the One for Me (Evan & Kendall)

Book 3: The Path to You (Everett & Bethany)

Book 4: Coming Home for Us (Elijah & Maddie)

Book 5: Stay Here With Me (East & Lark)

Book 6: Finding the Road to Us (Elliot, Trace, and Sidney)

Book 7: Moments for You (Ridge & Aurora)

Book 7.5: A Wilder Wedding (Amos & Naomi)

Book 8: Forever For Us (Wyatt & Ava)

Book 9: Pieces of Me (Gabriel & Briar)

Book 10: Endlessly Yours (Brooks & Rory)

NEXT IN THE WILDER BROTHERS SERIES:
Gabriel and Briar find out their path in PIECES OF ME.

IF YOU'D LIKE TO READ A BONUS SCENE
FEATURING AURORA & RIDGE:
CHECK OUT THIS SPECIAL EPILOGUE!

If you want to make sure you know what's coming next from me, you can sign up for my newsletter at www. CarrieAnnRyan.com; follow me on twitter at @CarrieAnnRyan, or like my Facebook page. I also have a Facebook Fan Club where we have trivia, chats, and

other goodies. You guys are the reason I get to do what
I do and I thank you.

Make sure you're signed up for my MAILING LIST so
you can know when the next releases are available as
well as find giveaways and FREE READS.

Happy Reading!

ALSO FROM CARRIE ANN RYAN

The Montgomery Ink Legacy Series:
   Book 1: Bittersweet Promises (Leif & Brooke)
   Book 2: At First Meet (Nick & Lake)
   Book 2.5: Happily Ever Never (May & Leo)
   Book 3: Longtime Crush (Sebastian & Raven)
   Book 4: Best Friend Temptation (Noah, Ford, and Greer)
   Book 4.5: Happily Ever Maybe (Jennifer & Gus)
   Book 5: Last First Kiss (Daisy & Hugh)
   Book 6: His Second Chance (Kane & Phoebe)
   Book 7: One Night with You (Kingston & Claire)
   Book 8: Accidentally Forever (Crew & Aria)

The Wilder Brothers Series:
   Book 1: One Way Back to Me (Eli & Alexis)

Book 2: Always the One for Me (Evan & Kendall)

Book 3: The Path to You (Everett & Bethany)

Book 4: Coming Home for Us (Elijah & Maddie)

Book 5: Stay Here With Me (East & Lark)

Book 6: Finding the Road to Us (Elliot, Trace, and Sidney)

Book 7: Moments for You (Ridge & Aurora)

Book 7.5: A Wilder Wedding (Amos & Naomi)

Book 8: Forever For Us (Wyatt & Ava)

Book 9: Pieces of Me (Gabriel & Briar)

Book 10: Endlessly Yours (Brooks & Rory)

The Cage Family

Book 1: The Forever Rule (Aston & Emma)

Book 2: An Unexpected Everything (Isabella & Weston)

The First Time Series:

Book 1: Good Time Boyfriend (Heath & Denver)

Book 2: Last Minute Fiancé (Luca & Addison)

Book 3: Second Chance Husband (August & Paisley)

The Montgomery Ink: Fort Collins Series:

Book 1: Inked Persuasion (Jacob & Annabelle)

Book 2: Inked Obsession (Beckett & Eliza)

Book 3: Inked Devotion (Benjamin & Brenna)

Book 3.5: Nothing But Ink (Clay & Riggs)

Book 4: Inked Craving (Lee & Paige)

Book 5: Inked Temptation (Archer & Killian)

The Montgomery Ink: Boulder Series:

Book 1: Wrapped in Ink (Liam & Arden)

Book 2: Sated in Ink (Ethan, Lincoln, and Holland)

Book 3: Embraced in Ink (Bristol & Marcus)

Book 3: Moments in Ink (Zia & Meredith)

Book 4: Seduced in Ink (Aaron & Madison)

Book 4.5: Captured in Ink (Julia, Ronin, & Kincaid)

Book 4.7: Inked Fantasy (Secret ??)

Book 4.8: A Very Montgomery Christmas (The Entire Boulder Family)

Montgomery Ink: Colorado Springs

Book 1: Fallen Ink (Adrienne & Mace)

Book 2: Restless Ink (Thea & Dimitri)

Book 2.5: Ashes to Ink (Abby & Ryan)

Book 3: Jagged Ink (Roxie & Carter)

Book 3.5: Ink by Numbers (Landon & Kaylee)

Montgomery Ink Denver:

Book 0.5: Ink Inspired (Shep & Shea)

Book 0.6: Ink Reunited (Sassy, Rare, and Ian)

Book 1: Delicate Ink (Austin & Sierra)

Book 1.5: Forever Ink (Callie & Morgan)

Book 2: Tempting Boundaries (Decker and Miranda)

Book 3: <u>Harder than Words</u> (Meghan & Luc)

Book 3.5: <u>Finally Found You</u> (Mason & Presley)

Book 4: <u>Written in Ink</u> (Griffin & Autumn)

Book 4.5: <u>Hidden Ink</u> (Hailey & Sloane)

Book 5: <u>Ink Enduring</u> (Maya, Jake, and Border)

Book 6: <u>Ink Exposed</u> (Alex & Tabby)

Book 6.5: <u>Adoring Ink</u> (Holly & Brody)

Book 6.6: <u>Love, Honor, & Ink</u> (Arianna & Harper)

Book 7: <u>Inked Expressions</u> (Storm & Everly)

Book 7.3: <u>Dropout</u> (Grayson & Kate)

Book 7.5: <u>Executive Ink</u> (Jax & Ashlynn)

Book 8: <u>Inked Memories</u> (Wes & Jillian)

Book 8.5: <u>Inked Nights</u> (Derek & Olivia)

Book 8.7: <u>Second Chance Ink</u> (Brandon & Lauren)

Book 8.5: Montgomery Midnight Kisses (Alex & Tabby Bonus(

Bonus: Inked Kingdom (Stone & Sarina)

The On My Own Series:

Book 0.5: My First Glance

Book 1: My One Night (Dillon & Elise)

Book 2: My Rebound (Pacey & Mackenzie)

Book 3: My Next Play (Miles & Nessa)

Book 4: My Bad Decisions (Tanner & Natalie)

The Promise Me Series:

Book 1: Forever Only Once (Cross & Hazel)

Book 2: From That Moment (Prior & Paris)

Book 3: Far From Destined (Macon & Dakota)

Book 4: From Our First (Nate & Myra)

The Less Than Series:

Book 1: Breathless With Her (Devin & Erin)

Book 2: Reckless With You (Tucker & Amelia)

Book 3: Shameless With Him (Caleb & Zoey)

The Fractured Connections Series:

Book 1: Breaking Without You (Cameron & Violet)

Book 2: Shouldn't Have You (Brendon & Harmony)

Book 3: Falling With You (Aiden & Sienna)

Book 4: Taken With You (Beckham & Meadow)

The Whiskey and Lies Series:

Book 1: Whiskey Secrets (Dare & Kenzie)

Book 2: Whiskey Reveals (Fox & Melody)

Book 3: Whiskey Undone (Loch & Ainsley)

The Gallagher Brothers Series:

Book 1: Love Restored (Graham & Blake)

Book 2: Passion Restored (Owen & Liz)

Book 3: Hope Restored (Murphy & Tessa)

The Ravenwood Coven Series:

Book 1: Dawn Unearthed

Book 2: Dusk Unveiled

Book 3: Evernight Unleashed

The Aspen Pack Series:

Book 1: Etched in Honor

Book 2: Hunted in Darkness

Book 3: Mated in Chaos

Book 4: Harbored in Silence

Book 5: Marked in Flames

The Talon Pack:

Book 1: <u>Tattered Loyalties</u>

Book 2: <u>An Alpha's Choice</u>

Book 3: <u>Mated in Mist</u>

Book 4: <u>Wolf Betrayed</u>

Book 5: <u>Fractured Silence</u>

Book 6: <u>Destiny Disgraced</u>

Book 7: <u>Eternal Mourning</u>

Book 8: <u>Strength Enduring</u>

Book 9: <u>Forever Broken</u>

Book 10: Mated in Darkness

Book 11: Fated in Winter

Redwood Pack Series:

Book 1: <u>An Alpha's Path</u>

Book 2: <u>A Taste for a Mate</u>

Book 3: <u>Trinity Bound</u>

Book 3.5: <u>A Night Away</u>

Book 4: <u>Enforcer's Redemption</u>

Book 4.5: <u>Blurred Expectations</u>

Book 4.7: <u>Forgiveness</u>

Book 5: <u>Shattered Emotions</u>

Book 6: <u>Hidden Destiny</u>

Book 6.5: <u>A Beta's Haven</u>

Book 7: <u>Fighting Fate</u>

Book 7.5: <u>Loving the Omega</u>

Book 7.7: <u>The Hunted Heart</u>

Book 8: <u>Wicked Wolf</u>

The Elements of Five Series:

Book 1: From Breath and Ruin

Book 2: From Flame and Ash

Book 3: From Spirit and Binding

Book 4: From Shadow and Silence

Dante's Circle Series:

Book 1: <u>Dust of My Wings</u>

Book 2: <u>Her Warriors' Three Wishes</u>

Book 3: <u>An Unlucky Moon</u>

Book 3.5: <u>His Choice</u>

Book 4: <u>Tangled Innocence</u>

Book 5: <u>Fierce Enchantment</u>

Book 6: <u>An Immortal's Song</u>

Book 7: <u>Prowled Darkness</u>

Book 8: Dante's Circle Reborn

Holiday, Montana Series:
Book 1: <u>Charmed Spirits</u>
Book 2: <u>Santa's Executive</u>
Book 3: <u>Finding Abigail</u>
Book 4: <u>Her Lucky Love</u>
Book 5: Dreams of Ivory

The Branded Pack Series:
(Written with Alexandra Ivy)
Book 1: <u>Stolen and Forgiven</u>
Book 2: <u>Abandoned and Unseen</u>
Book 3: <u>Buried and Shadowed</u>

ABOUT THE AUTHOR

Carrie Ann Ryan is the New York Times and USA Today bestselling author of contemporary, paranormal, and young adult romance. Her works include the Montgomery Ink, Redwood Pack, Fractured Connections, and Elements of Five series, which have sold over 3.0 million books worldwide. She started writing while in graduate school for her advanced degree in chemistry and hasn't stopped since. Carrie Ann has written over seventy-five novels and novellas with more in the works. When she's not losing herself in her emotional and action-packed worlds, she's reading as much as she can while wrangling her clowder of cats who have more followers than she does.

www.CarrieAnnRyan.com